HUSH, HUSH

A PRETTY LITTLE DEAD GIRL PREQUEL

E. M. MOORE

Pretty Little Dead Girl

Hush, Hush (Prequel)

Pretty Secrets

Rejected Mate Academy

Untamed

Forsaken

Saint Clary's University

Those Heartless Boys

This Fearless Girl

These Reckless Hearts

The Heights Crew Series

Uppercut Princess

Arm Candy Warrior

Beautiful Soldier

Knockout Queen

Crowned Crew (Heights POVs & Stories)

Finn

Jax

The Ballers of Rockport High Series

Game On

Foul Line

At the Buzzer

Rockstars of Hollywood Hill

Rock On

Spring Hill Blue Series

Free Fall

Catch Me

Ravana Clan Vampires Series

Chosen By Darkness

Into the Darkness

Falling For Darkness

Surrender To Darkness

Ravana Clan Legacy Series

A New Genesis

Tracking Fate

Cursed Gift

Veiled History

Fractured Vision

Chosen Destiny

Order of the Akasha Series

Stripped (Prequel)

Summoned By Magic

Tempted By Magic

Ravished By Magic

Indulged By Magic

Enraged By Magic

Her Alien Scouts Series

Kain Encounters

Kain Seduction

Safe Haven Academy Series

A Sky So Dark

A Dawn So Quiet

Chronicles of Cas Series

Reawakened

Hidden

Power

Severed

Rogue

The Adams' Witch Series

Bound In Blood

Cursed In Love

Witchy Librarian Cozy Mystery Series

Wicked Witchcraft

One Wicked Sister

Wicked Cool

Wicked Wiccans

The Mediterranean breeze kisses my skin, diluting the scorching heat of the sun's rays. Sparkles dance across rippling waves like glittering diamonds. In the distance, a speed boat motor roars as it nears. My sister, Eden, zooms by on water skis, skin glistening with small droplets. She waves, a gigantic smile on her face, before she holds tight to the rope again. I only shake my head at her as the previous soft crests of water turn tumultuous, making our boat bob up and down and to and fro in a rocking rhythm that could easily lull me to sleep—again.

The salt in the air coats me in a second skin, filling my nostrils with that delicious oceanic scent. There's something about the sea air that inspires me to do nothing, coaxing me into a dead weight of relaxation. It's heaven on earth. Naps are a part of everyday life while we cruise along the coast of Spain. Something I don't get at all when I'm back at school.

Taking a deep breath, I let it out in a slow exhale. The tropical wind quickly carries my worries away. The sunning deck on this huge boat is my oasis, and I take full advantage of it. My eyes shutter closed as I let the gentle movements of the vessel rock me into oblivion. At least, that was my plan.

The speed boat's engine growls, and I glance over to find Eden letting go of the rope that's responsible for pulling her along the surface. She skates over the water on two skis before falling amongst the waves right near the stern. She resurfaces, water clinging to her lashes. "Little help," she calls out.

Bliss still beckons, so I'm a little sluggish getting to my feet. Descending the ladder, I move to the next level before taking a set of curved stairs to grab an offered ski from Eden. She's already tossed the other on the deck and is pulling herself up. I give her a hand, knocking her other ski out of the way. "Thanks, Sis," she coos. Before I can dart out of the way, she throws her arms around me, laughing as she transfers her drenched skin to mine.

"You bitch," I giggle, hugging her right back. The water actually feels amazing against my heated body. I think I've toasted myself enough for now.

She fake gasps. "Did Princess Dee just curse?"

I peel her away playfully and halfheartedly punch her upper arm. "I guess the water is making me drunk."

"No, it's called rest and relaxation. Peace. You know, the things you don't feel because you have your head so far up your ass all the time." She gives me a winning smile afterward to soften the blow. Not that I take it as a negative, anyway.

"Ha. Ha," I deadpan. "I can't help it that I'm the golden child while you waste away at—"

"—some no name college where it's pure enjoyment all the time?" She drops back onto the seating area. Golden tanned, bare arms drape around the back of the couch. "Yeah, it's okay. I'll take what I got any day of the week."

I follow after her, sitting down on the opposite side of the couch and pulling my feet up to sprawl out. Using the arm as a headrest, I peer over at my sister with a half smile. I don't exactly envy Eden. It is what it is. I'm a first-born Astor, born to a first-born Astor. I have responsibilities that don't trickle down to her. It's been that way and will always be that way. I've never minded.

The deck hand that captained Eden's speed boat strides by, giving us both a respectful nod. "Thanks!" Eden calls out, giving him a quick wave. He raises his in return while she sits forward to peel off her life jacket, revealing a coral bikini underneath. She dangles the preserver in front of me. "You're sure I can't entice you?"

I lift my lip at it in disgust. I'm cool with boats, of cruising on top of the water, but do not ever expect me to get *in* the water. Can't do it. Won't do it. The view is so much better from up here anyway. Glitter-dusted blue green water for as far as the eye can see.

"Your tan's looking good anyway," she concedes, roaming her gaze across my newly bronzing skin in admiration. She plops the life jacket down on the deck to dry then relaxes backward onto the sofa cushions.

"It's something to take back with me to the Northeast when I return."

She mirrors the same look I gave her about the life jacket. Eden went to school in California. Her beach pictures are the only thing that can begin to make me jealous of her situation. The closest beaches to me are not what I consider fun in the sun.

Even though a year separates us, my sister and I could be twins. Our hair is the same blonde tone, though hers is a hair thicker than mine. She's also a couple of inches taller, a fact that annoys me to no end, especially when I was training ballet seriously. Her lines would be so pretty, but she never took to that particular discipline. *Too elitist*, she called it. I call it the echelon of grace and beauty, the physical art of what I want my life to look like—of what my life is expected to look like.

Eden darts a troubled gaze over her shoulder. "Where is he?"

I shrug, knowing she's talking about our father. "Somewhere on the boat. I mean, it's not *that* big."

Her lips thin, but her natural response flows easily from her mouth despite distraction. "He's going to kill you if he hears you say *boat* again."

"Yeah, but yacht sounds so pretentious."

Eden still roams her gaze over this level. From here, we can see through the dining room into the gigantic kitchen. Another deckhand, a chef this time, is preparing a spread for our guests that should be arriving shortly. When she doesn't find our father, she turns back to me. "You're the most conscientious rich person I know."

"We're not rich—"

"Yeah, yeah. *Our parents* are rich. You don't have to tell me."

I snicker. "Don't act like you actually believe I should go around talking about how I spent my break on a yacht just off the coast of Spain." I cast my gaze off the edges of the vessel, spying a smattering of white objects in the water. Some closer, some far away. "There are more than a few Carnegie students doing the exact same thing we are. No one cares."

She huffs. "Yes, but you try to downplay it like it's no big deal."

"And you don't? Do you walk around campus talking about being on 'daddy's yacht' during break?"

"Of course not, but I'm not going to school with millionaires. It's pretty much expected of you at Carnegie, isn't it?"

Shrugging, I dutifully ignore her attempts to pull me into a debate. I don't think our money is dirty like she does but flaunting it when I'm not the one who earned it makes me uncomfortable. I've always felt the need to prove myself as an Astor. Eden's the same way except with one major difference: she'd rather not be an Astor at all.

Instead of allowing her to lure me in, I close my eyes and let the sun's heat and the soft rolling of the boat relax me again.

"I hope Dad stops fucking his mistress before the Forbes get here."

I open one eye, glaring at her. The heavy tint on my sunglasses does nothing to erase the furious expression on her face though. The older she got and the more she saw, her distrust of our world heightened. "I'm sure he will," I tell her, trying not to think about our father in bed with one of the female deckhands. When I was ten, and first discovered one of my father's lurid affairs, I divulged the secret to Eden. We marched into our mother's room and told her every-thing we knew, expecting something monumental to happen. A fight. An argument. By telling her, we thought she'd get him to stop.

The exact opposite happened. She did nothing, and he still continues to philander with anyone who has a nice size chest and a decent pair of legs. In fact, our mother's not even on this trip, probably to allow him time to sow his oats or whatever disgustingly ridiculous excuse she gives him.

I won't live like that. I'll put up with a lot by being an Astor, but a cheating spouse isn't one of them. I want a partner for life.

"You're so casual about it," Eden fumes.

I sit up, cross my legs, and stare at the near image of myself with one big difference. Eden has always had a fire in her eyes that I lacked. A spark. An impassioned sense of right and wrong. Me? I just try to do better to deserve all the accolades my family gets. "Eden..."

"Delilah..." she drones as if she's already preparing for my lame speech. Crossing her arms, she peers away, jaw working. A second later, she gives me an apologetic smile.

I cling to that grin, hating that she's so affected by what our parents do. Their actions are not ours. "You know I don't like it either. There's nothing we can do about it. Dad's not going to change anytime soon. Plus, what he does in his spare time has no impact on his feelings for us."

"Did you read that in a self-help book?"

I smirk at her. "No, my therapist."

"Even better."

I watch as she mulls over my words, biting her inner lip. "Seriously, though. Dad loves you. Dad loves me. Let him and Mom deal with their crap."

She huffs, but she's a little lighter now. "He should realize we're smart enough to understand what's going on. He acts like we're still little girls."

I'm not sure I get the difference. Even if he hid his transgressions better, he'd still be doing it. Either way, though, what he does is not my responsibility to worry about.

"Speaking of guys being dicks," Eden helpfully changes the subject. "I bet you can't wait to see Keegan."

My stomach clenches at his name. Keegan Forbes. Only the handsomest man I've ever met. He was the cutest boy on the playground, and he only got better with age. Dimples. Muscles. A smile that could talk your panties off in a heartbeat.

The problem with Keegan is, he knows he's hot stuff and takes advantage of it whenever he wants.

I have a love/hate relationship with him. As in, I've loved him my whole life, from the moment he dragged me out of his family's pool lifeless when I was just four years old, until now. There are times when I've hated him. Except, that's not completely accurate. It's more like I hate that I love him. He's chauvinistic, cocky, and his ego knows no bounds. However, the Keegan I know is a generous, kind person. He's just hidden beneath some very unsexy traits right now.

"You know, you don't have to marry him," Eden states firmly.

My cheeks blush. A rush of simultaneous panic and want flutters over my skin. "We're not engaged."

Rolling her eyes, she sighs. "You know what I mean. You can have anyone you want, business decisions be damned."

Eden's never liked Keegan. At first I thought it was jealousy, but I'm pretty sure it's because he represents everything she doesn't like about being a descendant of old money, of being a caretaker to fortunes regular people can only dream of. He's proud. He's self-centered. And let's face it, he's coddled.

I'm just waiting for him to grow up, blossom into his true potential. Eden thinks I'm blinded by duty. The Forbes and the Astors have an understanding, an agreement that Keegan and I will end up together, thereby expanding our wealth. I've never minded. He saved my life, after all.

"I know I can make my own decisions," I tell her

honestly, thinking back on mine and Keegan's tumultuous history. He was my first kiss. My first dance partner. The first boy to make me stay up all night crying. He's a lot more to me than just the guy my parents expect me to wed. "Just be lucky he didn't have a younger brother, so you're safe," I joke.

"Are you kidding?" she laughs. "We're never safe. I'm pretty sure Mom still has a hard-on for me and Oliver."

"Do mom's get hard-ons?"

She leans back, shrugging. "If they do, Mom has one for me and my best friend."

Methinks she might be protesting too much, but she's also so hyper focused away from anyone with money that she could be overlooking him all together. It's clear her "best friend" likes her. "That's because Oliver is a prince and has a British accent. She probably thinks your little Astor heirs will run around with accents too."

"He's not even an important prince," she bemoans, rolling her eyes into the back of her head. "Though, the accent thing would be pretty cool."

Unlike my sister, I let it drop. I'm not going to involve myself in her love life. She'll figure it out. She always does.

A member of the kitchen staff stops in front of us, her hands clasped in front. "The table is arranged with hors d'oeuvres. Is there anything you would like me to do before your guests arrive?"

I peek over my shoulder to find the nicest arrangement of fruits, meats, and desserts that would actually be considered a full-fledged meal for most people. "Thank you. It looks wonderful," I tell her. "I don't think we'll be needing more."

"Thank you, miss. Also, your father would like me to tell you that the Forbes have radioed and are on their way over now." I smile as she walks away, retreating into the interior of the yacht where she'll make herself scarce, but also ever ready in case we need her for some sort of culinary emergency.

I place my hand over my stomach as it twists. I peer in both directions and spot a shiny dinghy making its way toward us. Two posh figures stand inside, holding onto the canopied roof for support as the vessel cuts through the waves. The closer it gets, the clearer Keegan becomes. Like usual, he's dashing, effortlessly handsome. It's been two weeks since we were together back at Carnegie, back in the clutches of the Knights, but it feels like only yesterday.

My current relationship with Keegan is non-existent. He's not happy I decided to join *his* prestigious club, the Knights of Arcadia. The way I see it though, membership is my birthright just as it is his. Plus, being a Knight brings me that much closer to being worthy of everything the Astors have.

Knights rule the world—literally. And if I want to be anyone, I have to be one. I'll carry on the traditions of my father, now an elder of the secret group, as well as his father before him. The Knights are nothing if not steeped in tradition.

Part of that tradition is remaining mysterious. The group's existence isn't hidden, however, the members and their doings are. Their practices, the meetings, everything that happens behind the scenes is so hush-hush, flying completely under the radar. If the world only knew that the Knights were basically in control of almost everything that happened in this world, the divide between the haves and have-nots would be so utterly obvious that chaos would ensue.

I want to make sure that never happens while also taking control of my birthright as a proud Knight.

If only Keegan saw it that way.

2

Keegan and his father together are too much testosterone to take. Their stares linger far longer than necessary when we greet them, welcoming them onto the Leona III. Their similar, striking blue eyes eat us up predatorily. When father arrives from somewhere within the belly of his prized possession, Eden walks off, returning a few minutes later dressed in a sundress.

I can't even blame her.

At school, Keegan is distant and aloof, his poor little rich boy pride hurt when I became a fledgling Knight at the same time he did. Men in my world don't see women as equals. My father had to petition the Arcadian elders to allow me into their good ol' boy society. I don't know this for sure, but I imagine it took some convincing, and based solely on how I've been treated thus far, I'm certain not everyone voted in my father's favor. The fact is, my parents didn't birth a male heir. Though that might seem almost criminal in some well-to-do families, it is what it is, and Alistair Astor was not going to let his Arcadian legacy die with him.

In that, I can always be proud of my father. He's always told me there's zero difference between me and the myriad of driven men I'm surrounded by daily. If I want something, I can't let a little thing like gender inequality get in my way. He may have given me the opportunity to make it into the Knights of Arcadia, but *I'm* the one who surpassed their trials and came out unscathed.

I shiver at the memories, darting my gaze to Keegan who's ogling my cleavage and not even pretending to do otherwise. He's dressed in a crisp, white shirt over khaki shorts, looking every bit the sun-kissed, rich guy. I should've followed Eden's lead earlier and changed because Mr. Forbes is just as bad, but he at least has the decency to hide it in front of my dad. The elder Forbes swings his polo shirt clad arm around my shoulders, fingertips dancing down my upper arm. His shorts are a pleated blue. The combination of polo and fancy shorts, backdropped by a yacht, makes it look like he stole the captain's uniform and decided to wear it out for the day.

"How's sweet Delilah? Keegan says you're excelling at Carnegie."

"I'm well. Thank you, Sir." I don't bother going into specifics. I learned a long time ago that when important men get together, they don't wish to have females drone on about anything they believe you shouldn't be educated in. Business? Economics? No, I'm just here to look good on Keegan's arm. The face of poise, grace, and well-bred civility. Honestly, it's kind of like being a thoroughbred racehorse.

I'm going to change all that though.

He squeezes me into his side, my breasts smashing together. He takes his fill while my father is turned away, pouring brandy into crystal decanters. Eden immediately cuts in. "Dee, the sun's going down. You should change out of that suit."

I eye her gratefully as Leon Forbes releases his hold. Sometimes, it's difficult to wrangle out of his grasp. Once, I was forced to stand by his side for a whole two hours during Keegan's high school graduation celebration. I spent more time with his father that day than I did with Keegan himself. Leon Forbes holds the reins tight, just like he operates in the boardroom of his Fortune 500 company. "Of course." His smile tightens. "We wouldn't want you to get sick for the start of the next semester."

"No, Sir. We don't."

Turning, I make it two steps before Keegan is at my side, following me into the other room. "Damn, Dee. Sometimes I forget how much you've grown."

My cheeks heat at his praise. At Carnegie, he hardly looks at me. In fact, these are the nicest words he's spoken to me in months. An unwitting smile pulls my lips apart as I meet his gaze. I don't want him to want me for my body, but I also can't stop the race of hormones his words conjure. From day one, I've only ever sought Keegan's affection.

We've been on again off again our entire lives. When we were kids, we were just friends. Then we went into pre-teen years where feelings were so new and awkward. We didn't understand the emotions roiling through us. Though Keegan seemed to understand them well before me. He invited me to be his date for his first prep school dance, giving me my first kiss under an array of colorful streamers and twinkling garden lights. We broke up the following week because he'd found a girl at his own school to date.

When we got older, we understood the agreement between our families. We tried again when we were both in private school, but it was obvious Keegan was much more informed than I was about dating and relationships. Well, *certain* areas of being in a relationship. For everything he did know, he didn't know how to actually be a boyfriend. He wanted me, the Astor heir, and whoever else he decided to sleep with on the side. The day a girl messaged me on social media that she'd slept with him at a party broke my heart.

From that day forward, our relationship has been more of a show than anything else. I've been biding my time, waiting for him to mature into the man I know he can be. I don't want a piece of Keegan Forbes. I want him, heart and soul. Until he's ready for that, we can play this game of back and forth, of pretending in front of people, but I won't give him my whole heart until he deserves it.

"You haven't been looking," I chastise, fully facing him now so he can see what he's not getting. I'm a feminist, but I also know when to work my assets. I purposefully wore this bikini today because I knew I'd get a reaction out of him. He's basically motivated only by tits, ass, and not disappointing his father.

"Jealous?" he mocks, his pearly whites coming out to grin at me as if he's ensnared me in his web.

I make a snorting sound in the back of my throat. "Not in the least," I respond, hoping I sound convincing. I really am jealous, actually. I don't understand why I can't be enough for Keegan. If we're going to eventually end up together, why can't he just do it now? On the other hand, I give him some major slack because the world we grew up in promotes his behavior. Since his father is the worst offender, I knew he'd want to have his cake and eat it too. Hell, even my own father thinks he deserves anything and everything. Willpower isn't something this world practices enough.

He glowers, gaze darkening until his eyes are a stormy blue. Now, this is the part of Keegan I'm used to. "You're always so stuck up. Being an Astor isn't everything."

I beg to differ. To me, being an Astor is *everything*. "The fact that your mind went there proves how little you know about females."

Keegan leans on the gleaming white railing next to us. He's the picture of relaxation, but his words are sour and hateful. "The fact that I could fuck you right here, right now, and no one would say a damn thing except to congratulate us means you're the one living in some fantasy land, Dee."

Color drains from my face, settling in the pit of my stomach. He's absolutely right. Eden would pitch a fit, of course, but our fathers would be over the moon, most likely staring at my stomach afterward as if an heir could magically appear from just one cum squirt.

He licks his lips, gaze drawing downward as he inspects every inch of my body. "You should get off your high horse, baby factory. One day soon, I'm going to fuck you so hard you're going to be begging me to fill you over and over and over..."

His words rake over me. Unwanted heat pools in

my belly. The image of him finally taking me repeats in my head as my breath hitches. How can I simultaneously be turned on *and* want to slap him? Because he knows just how to get under my skin, that's how. I stuff the desire aside and tiptoe my fingers up his arm. "Maybe we'll wait until science figures out how men can carry babies. We'll certainly be able to afford it."

His blue eyes flash, and I swear he's getting off on this. It's as if backtalk and verbal sparring are precursors to sex in his world. "I can occupy that smart mouth with something better." His eyes gleam. "Or I can go back to the girl I fucked yesterday. And this morning. And this afternoon." He pulls me to the side of the yacht that faces East. He points to a bobbing boat in the distance. I can just make out the fact that it has Keegan's family name scrawled across the bow. Leaning over, he presses his lips against the shell of my ear. His hot breath curls my toes. "She didn't mind me going in bareback..." He kisses my ear, sucking the lobe between his teeth. "...three times." He bites down, tugging until he rakes his teeth free. "Maybe she'll carry my heir."

The worst part about playing his game is that Keegan knows I love him. He understands the buttons to push, wielding them to his benefit. What's uncertain is whether those feelings are reciprocated.

A lithe figure stands on his yacht's sunning area,

and my blood boils. That's definitely not Mrs. Forbes. This woman is about three sizes smaller with a waist that looks like it's been taken in by a corset. The woman could be either his or his father's. Or both, I suppose. I turn toward him, hiding the fact that I just had to lock my heart away so I don't crumble in front of him. "You're sick, you know that?"

"Oh, come on, Delilah. You act like you want to play big boy games, let's play big boy games. You're a Knight, after all. Cunning. Brave. Fier—"

Eden wiggles herself to my side. She glares at Keegan. "I don't know what's going on here, but you better leave my sister the fuck alone."

His grin only widens. "Aww, Eden. You're always so feisty. I bet you'd be fun in the sack. A lot more exciting than your ice queen sister. You can suck good dick, can't you?" His stare drops to my sister's lips.

She curls them into a cruel smirk. "If I'm ever that close to your balls, I'm cutting them off." Her smile turns innocent as she calls out, "Isn't that right, Daddy?"

My father spins, giving us a short, two-fingered wave. "That's right, Honey."

I chuckle. Okay, maybe he can be a little too supportive, especially when he doesn't realize what he's agreeing to. He's already turned back toward Leon

Forbes, giving his slick, black hair a comb through with his fingers while the breeze threatens to upend it.

Eden guides me away, right through the glass doors that lead to the dining room and kitchen. As soon as the doors close behind me, I'm swamped by air conditioning. A shiver runs through me as my heated skin meets the artificial chill. Goosebumps sprout up and down my body, then stay when I replay the interaction I just had with Keegan.

It wouldn't surprise me if he is fucking another girl just a few hundred yards away from me. I bet he gets off on doing that. He certainly gets off on throwing it in my face. He wants me to be jealous because he thinks that if I am, I'll drop my panties for him in a second as some sort of ridiculous attempt to win his affection.

Sex is the only thing I've been able to hold back from him. Once we go there, there's no turning back. It's my last bargaining chip in trying to keep me ahead of the game that, as he so animatedly pointed out, I'm so bad at playing. It's also the one thing he would do anything for.

He told me once in one of his rare, raw moments that he dreams about taking that one last thing from me. My purity. The fact that he'll be the first to go there excites him to no end. I believe it's the one thing that actually keeps him coming back. He can get laid anywhere. He can get dirty and screw as much as his black heart desires. But the one thing he can't get from them, that I have, is my fully intact sex. He's more reverent of that than my actual heart.

Furthering my hypothesis, I also believe it's one of the main reasons why he just hasn't made me yet. As he callously remarked, he could fuck me on a table in front of everyone, and no one would care about what I'd just lost. They'd just be excited that we'd finally come together.

I'm keeping this bargaining chip locked up until I decide to give it away. For me. Not because I'm supposed to. Not because he wants it. But because I do.

Knowing that, I take the hallway to the curving stairs that lead to the staterooms below deck. As Eden suggested, I change out my attire for a less revealing sundress.

I've poked the grumpy bear enough for today.

Unfortunately, Keegan's never done with me.

3

*D*inner goes smoothly. Our fathers talk business, throwing around names that are familiar only because they've been discussed in front of me hundreds of times before, and possibly because I met them at some soiree when I was a teenager. Businessmen love to hobnob.

Keegan goes through spurts of fitting right in with the two elders, offering his welcomed two cents before zoning out again. I eye him through most of the meal, wondering what happened to him. What made that little boy who saved my life grow up to be this thing sitting next to me.

No matter the hurt he's caused, I can't find it in me to hate him. Eden thinks it's a major flaw in my personality to still be attracted to the guy who's already broken my heart a few times. Also, the fact that I haven't told Mom and Dad—and their arrangement with the Forbes—to eff off perturbs her to no end. I'm resilient like that though. I'm not going to admit I was dumb until Keegan forces my hand.

After dinner, our fathers take over the dining room table to play cards for sums of money I don't even want to think about. Keegan opts to retire to the salon with Eden and me where we watch mind-numbing TV until Eden starts to doze. It's a wonder she lasted this long. While I was napping most of the day, she was out exploring the water like she does—snorkeling, swimming, water skiing. I nudge her with my arm. She blinks awake suddenly, focusing on me and then beyond where Keegan still sits before she frowns.

"Don't feel like you have to stay up for me," I tell her. "I'm fine."

Our fathers' cigar smoke has filled the room with a heavy scent. The lull of the rocking yacht is enough to make anyone fall asleep, but I never let time slip by like that when I'm with Keegan. "You sure?" she asks, darting mistrusting eyes toward the other figure in the room who's leaning against the arm of the couch looking bored as ever. Honestly, he's always been easiest to take one-on-one, away from other people where he thinks he has to be a certain type of person to be respected.

"Yeah, of course."

She stands, covering a yawn. "I'll see you in the morning then." Before she walks away, she wavers a bit, assessing the situation. She got my father's evaluating nature, that's for sure. Eventually, she spins on her heel and walks down the curved stairs toward her private stateroom.

With Keegan and I alone, it's hard to remember what he said to me before dinner. I've already claimed ownership over him in my head, chalking up his mistakes to the world we were raised in where we want for nothing.

It was the same for me when I was young. Most little princesses ask for ponies, and I did the same. My classmates and I all had them—several, even. It was only from watching programs on television that I noticed it wasn't like that for everyone. Middle class families didn't get the revolutionary new gadget that just hit the stores or a brand new phone the minute they got a cracked screen. They didn't go to expensive schools and play sports that cost more than some people's cars. We were spoiled, there's no other way around saying it. Only, some of us mature faster than others and realize that we shouldn't keep taking advantage of our parents' wealth. Instead, we should do something with our own.

"Your sister's out of control," Keegan bites out. He scowls toward the curved staircase where Eden retreated. "Your dad should do something about her." He changes the channel on the television a little too forcefully, smashing his finger into the remote.

Eden's the black sheep of the Astor family. I fight for her constantly, but no one else understands why she's determined to distance herself from the rest of us. "She's fine, actually," I reply. "She has a 4.0. She competes competitively in swimming and field hockey. She—"

"It's cute that you always defend her," he interrupts. "She doesn't want anything to do with your family now, but one of these days, she'll come around, begging for money. Trust me."

Just his word choice makes my hackles rise. I'm not being *cute*. "I think it's great that she wants to make it on her own."

"You would," he says dismissively, the pure sass in his tone making my hands turn to fists. "She won't be getting anything from us."

I dissect his words. Surely, he doesn't mean that even *if* we get together that *he* gets to say whether or not I give someone in my own family money. It's supposed to be a joining of fortunes, not the Forbes taking over what's ours.

I sigh because I just don't know what to do with him yet. His thinking is skewed, fueled by his father's chauvinism.

To add insult to injury, he glares at me before saying, "I can't wait to live with that sigh for the rest of my life."

Whoa. Rude. The face I see isn't the same as the boy who told me he *liked me, liked me* when we were ten. He's not the one who used to share everything with me. "I don't think you understand how cruel you can sound sometimes."

"I do. It's my specialty." He grins lifelessly at me. There's no passion behind his words, just muted indifference. I don't know which is worse. That he doesn't like me right now, or that he doesn't care enough to even feel that much. I give him some space, moving further away from him on the couch, but that just infuriates him further. "You know what's fucked up?" He tosses the remote onto the glass coffee table in front of us. "The fact that I have every other girl throwing themselves into my lap, and the girl I'm supposed to marry can't even stand being next to me." He eyes the distance between us like he wishes he could set it on fire. Instead, he bridges it, imposing himself on me.

Slinking closer, he runs his hand up my leg. I scoot away, but the arm of the couch stops me from going further. Keegan has that determined look in his eye as he pushes my leg out of the way to press his body between my thighs. My breath hitches at the contact. I hate when he gets this close. It's hard not to want things from him. "Is this just about sex?" I squeak.

"I have a dick. Of course it's about sex." He trails his palm up the inside of my calf, passes over my knee and then starts toward my upper thigh. I can't close my legs because he's currently between them. There's no way to escape. My dress gets caught in his forward movement, so every inch he gains up my leg, the skirt of my dress goes with him. He hitches the hem over my hip, displaying my panties for him. "You want to know what I think? I think you secretly want me. You secretly love that I want to fuck you so hard you won't be able to walk right away. Should I check your panties to find out?"

Dear God. I start to tremble. He skims his fingers closer, my muscles jumping underneath his touch. I already feel moisture seeping through my folds. I place my hand on his to stop him from going further, but he shakes it off.

"You're still intact for me, aren't you, Delilah?" Brushing his fingertips across the lining of my panties, he glues his eyes to the pink lace. When I don't answer, he gazes up at me expectantly. I wonder what he would do if I said no. It would be a complete lie, but still. "It's a simple question," he prods.

"Of course," I tell him, my breath coming out on an impassioned huff that's evidence of how much he's affecting me. Virginity isn't part of the deal for our parents. I can screw whoever I want, as can he. It's *my* thing. This picture-perfect ideal I have of the way things should be between Keegan and me.

His answering smirk makes me wish I'd told him no. It makes me want to find one of the crew members on this ship and just get it over with. The one thing that gives me power also makes Keegan's head balloon up to three times its size.

He trails a finger down the center of the pink lace. "There it is," he muses. I don't need to look down to know that the dampness coming from me must be showing through my panties. My hips ache to buck toward him, but I keep them firmly in place. "To know this untouched pussy is waiting for me..." A rumble edges from the back of his throat. "This pure cunt you've been hiding. I *need* it, Delilah." Slipping his finger just underneath the edge, he pulls the fabric of my panties away to run his finger along the inside seam. Chilled air passes over my core, making my muscles lock up. He hasn't even touched me and I'm already breathless.

Pulling my panties further away, he lets go, making them snap back into place. I suck in a breath at the sting. Instead of hurting, however, it does the opposite. Immediately, I try to distract myself. "Why are you so obsessed with sex?"

He flits the pad of his thumb over my panty line. "You say that because you haven't ridden my cock."

Excitement pours over me. If he could just promise he'd be the man I need him to be, I'd ride him right now. If he'd tell me he'd accept me as an equal, as his partner moving forward, I'd impale myself on his cock like I've dreamed about. "Did you really fuck some girl just this morning?"

Trailing his finger down the center of my panties once more, he peers up. "Dee, I do what I want. The sooner you learn that, the better." He licks his lips, returning his stare to my clothed core like a tiger on the prowl. "Like right now, I'm going to prove to you that you want me." He peels the pink lace aside, revealing my pussy. He eyes it like a drug, and I swear I can feel my heart beat where his gaze is fixated.

"Keegan, don't," I warn. My body has already taken control though. Muscles locked into place, I can feel his breath fan over my sensitive flesh. My pussy contracts, waiting to see what he'll do.

"Afraid I'll uncover your secret?" He blows across my drenched folds, and a shiver runs through me. Teasingly, he draws his fingers over my skin, slowly closing in on their destination one excruciating centimeter at a time.

I don't say anything. Poised in the middle between meaning to tell him to knock it off to being intensely curious as to how far he'll take this, I just stay where I am. He hasn't touched me like this in too damn long.

He flicks his gaze up. I have no doubt my cheeks are flushed. My jaw is slack, breath held tightly in my chest in preparation for the first contact. I look nothing like someone who's trying to fight him off. In fact, I'm just the opposite. He wets his lips. "You're beautiful."

Warring emotions aside, I melt at his words. I'm so focused on him that I don't realize he's getting closer to his intended target until he makes contact. I gasp. "Keegan."

Surprise flashes in his eyes as he circles his fingers over my pussy. "That's right. You want it. Dripping wet, Dee." His slow movements drive me mad. A ticking noise sounds in the background, and I anxiously look over my shoulder to make sure our fathers aren't witness to this. He brings my attention back to him by murmuring my name. "Delilah..." Turning, I find his fingers in his mouth, licking my juices from his skin.

"Oh God," I breathe, zooming in on his glistening fingertips. I'm enthralled, so caught up in the moment that my body starts shaking.

"Maybe you'll be a freak yet," he whispers. One last lick of his tongue and he's zeroing in on my core again. He inches closer, spending a few moments circling before pushing his finger past my folds.

I mute a strangled cry. Our fathers are just in the other room. Like he said, they wouldn't care. They'd be proud, and his father would most likely want to watch.

Thankfully, Keegan brings me back from that thought. "So warm, perfect." His hips start making small movements against my leg. His restraint is costing him a lot right now, that I can tell. However, his excitement heightens my own. My hips start to move with him, seeking out his finger as he dips it inside. "You like that, don't you? You love it, Dee. You want me so fucking much, you can't stand it."

My body starts to move without inhibition, pushing forward so I meet the thrusts of his fingers faster.

"Say it, Delilah. Admit it to yourself."

I press my lips together. The only thing I can think about is how good this feels. How much I have craved him over the years, ever since I understood what these feelings were. My traitorous body works with his. He's really going after it, propelling his finger forward, circling it inside, before pulling out in a rhythm that has me gobsmacked. My head drops back to the arm of the couch as I expel a soft cry.

"Say you'll fuck me."

My gaze snaps to his. He's not even looking at me. He's staring at my pussy in reverence. I try to grip his wrist. "We should stop."

His movements stutter before he lifts guarded eyes to me. "Stop? Don't fool yourself. You were just creaming all over me. Give me more."

"Keegan," I warn as he dives forward with new purpose. I make a small cry as he hits a spot inside me that almost makes stars appear in front of my eyes.

"There. Give it to me."

"Keegan, this isn't right," I protest, but my hips tell a different story. They're seeking the obvious pleasure he's building inside.

"Don't be scared," he murmurs, and his tone is almost soft.

"I'm— I'm not—"

He places the pad of his thumb on my clit and pushes down.

"Keegan!"

All rational thought obliterates within that span. My hips jump up to meet him, thrusting over his fingers as he flicks my clit. "Fuck, little princess. Go after it."

I do. With abandon. Climax is in sight, and I chase it with everything I have. Mouth wide open in ecstasy, harsh breaths filling the space, I go after what I want until I reach it. My pussy clenches around his finger as pleasure skates through my entire body. My toes curl, lost in triumphant bliss.

Eyes closed, I slump backward on the arm of the

couch, reveling in the sensations. It's as if time stops for a moment of beautiful languidity. However, the harsh sound of a zipper lowering forcefully grabs my attention. My lids fly open, revealing Keegan shoving his pants down his hips, his erect dick straining against his boxers.

Scrambling backward, the joy of the moment obliterates into surprise. "Keegan, what are you doing?"

"Fucking you. That's what I'm doing."

I throw myself over the arm of the couch and ungracefully land on my feet. "No."

His face shifts from confusion, to surprise, to anger within the span of three seconds.

He lifts himself from the couch, carefully replaces his shorts back on his hips, and with utter control, zips his zipper. "You're a fucking cock tease. You'll always be a fucking cock tease." Moving next to me, he stares down his nose as if he's on a whole other echelon. "You'll pay for that."

He runs into my shoulder as he leaves the room. I catch my balance, heart in my throat. If I didn't know any better, I'd believe I just saw the face of the devil in Keegan's eyes.

Carnegie University's campus is about as old world as you can get. The stone buildings jut into the sky with medieval-esque prominence. The architecture is intricate and bold. It's not far-fetched to imagine my four times great grandfather walking the same cobblestone pathways when he was my age.

The sprawling campus grounds, usually lush and green, are dotted with fallen leaves from the beautiful fall foliage northern New York is known for. Bright oranges, yellows, and reds make for a kaleidoscope of colors, accenting the stone buildings. It's like I'm walking through an Autumn magazine where everything is staged to inspire the reader, except this is real life. The only thing missing is the aroma of pumpkin spice, which I will happily get later at the campus' coffee bar.

Tucked away in the northeastern United States, Carnegie University isn't known to many. We don't have the same name recognition as Yale and Harvard unless your net worth is an acceptable figure. Among the elite of the elite, Carnegie is the only college to attend, especially when you have a pedigree like mine. My family has been attending Carnegie since the late 1600's when it was founded. I've been visiting this campus my whole life. Alumni luncheons and parties, grand openings of technology buildings and so forth. There's even an Astor Residence Hall that was named for my family after my great grandfather donated a hefty sum of money back into the university.

Nestled amongst the educational buildings is another layer that not all who attend the prestigious school are privy to; an organization that lies in wait to transform the path of our country's most powerful young minds. Carnegie University has a low acceptance rate, but an even bigger challenge is gaining membership into the Knights of Arcadia. Like with enrollment into Carnegie, your last name will help you, but it doesn't do everything. Everyone has to be up to the task, no matter their background.

I'm proud to be the first female member. I like to envision myself on a bulldozer, barreling over obstacles for the next wave of women to finally make it into this old boys' club because why shouldn't we have the same opportunities as our male counterparts?

Honestly, I should've majored in feminism, but like Carnegie would offer anything as groundbreaking as that as a concentration.

With school break well behind me, I'm looking forward to getting back into the daily grind. The Knights keep us newbies on our toes, and not to mention with my strict academic schedule, I can't afford to have my head sun-bleached right now. Carnegie has a strict GPA enforcement and my duties for the Knights will be ramping up as they put us through our paces. We may have been accepted already, but to become a fully-fledged Knight, we have to leave Carnegie with our standing intact. Not everyone does, and since I'll be the only one with breasts in the room, I'm pretty sure I'll be on their radar as someone they might have an easier time stripping knighthood from.

I always knew my journey would be an uphill battle but seeing Keegan over break brought everything back into perspective. Not to sound like my little sister, but the level of entitlement here is astronomical. So much so that Keegan doesn't think he has to work at being a boyfriend. He thinks I should just bend over and take it because he wants it.

My face flushes at the thought. I'm not going to

pretend I didn't like what we did together the other night because that would be a lie. However, my feelings are why I have to stand strong. I'll never gain his respect if I just do what he wants. I wasn't raised that way. Success comes from hard work, and in my opinion, he hasn't put in the effort to get between my legs. Just being hot doesn't gain you free access.

Pushing through the arched shaped door of my cozy residence hall, I drag my bag up over my shoulder as I enter the narrow, wooden steps that lead to my room. Each residence hall is unique and far removed from what other college campus's boast. The buildings are old but remodeled in the traditional vein. Every student has their own suite upstairs while the downstairs is set up with a common living area and kitchen. The buildings are basically moderately sized mansions, sleeping up to fifteen students. The men and women are separated. CU rules, of course, but that doesn't mean there isn't a lot of bed-hopping going on.

I use my key to enter my room, taking a moment to breathe it in. I've loved my time here at Carnegie. Not that I don't also love being at home, but since this is where I aspired to attend school even as a little girl, being here means something to me. The girls in my hall are great. The professors are extremely smart and humble. The education is second to none, especially with our small class sizes. The Knights of Arcadia is just the cherry on top.

In a year from now, I'll be thrown out into the real world, spearheading and growing my father's hospitality business. Carnegie, and my connections with the Knights, will help me successfully navigate the transition.

I swing my bag onto my bed and start unpacking. Of course, the bikinis and tank tops are going right back into storage. It's chilly here already. No more falling asleep to the heat of the sun on my face. Soon, I'll be feeling the biting cold wind whip against my cheeks.

Tucking my overnight bag under my bed, I'm just about to plop onto it, stretching out this moment of freedom before school starts again tomorrow when my phone starts buzzing repeatedly. I fish it out of my pocket and watch as texts come in from Keegan one after the other.

Call coming in

4

3

2

Confusion gives way to shock when my mother's name pops up on the screen as an incoming call. I stare at her profile pic, wondering what the hell Keegan has to do with this before answering the video chat.

I hold the phone away at arm's length, smiling tightly at the screen. "Hey, Mom."

She's staring down when the call first connects. The phone jostles, distorting the view for a moment before she rights it.

As she gets settled, I say, "I was about to call you. I just put away my clothes."

Finally, she stretches the phone out and puts it on a flat surface. At the very bottom of the screen, I spy the white iron bistro set that's set up in the garden back home. Tall bushes flank her all around. Out of shot are a line of manicured flowers. It's odd. Now that I can see her, I can almost feel being there, too. The way the wind filters through the garden, bringing with it the sweet scents of her massive array of flowers.

She adjusts the wide brim hat on her head. "That's good, sweetie. Did you have fun on vacation?"

Guilt presses into me, but it's more my own worries than hers. She knows my father cheats. She doesn't put up a fuss about it, so I don't know why Eden and I are the ones that get bent out of shape about it. I feel like I have to tell her every time he does, even though the chances of her not knowing are very slim. "It was great," I tell her. "It was good to hang out with Eden before she heads across the country again."

"I missed both of you guys," she announces. "But

hopefully I'll see you soon. Maybe I can come by some time for a lunch date when you're not busy, Delilah."

"Of course," I tell her. "Anytime." I sit at my desk chair, using the top to support my elbow as I continue to hold the phone out to make sure I'm still in frame. We both know she won't be coming to visit me, but it is a nice offer.

"Do you have a moment for me to talk to you about something?"

My brows contract as I try to take stock of her current mood. I notice she's really trying to stay as loose as possible, but it's all a facade. Anxiety spreads through my limbs as I realize something is up. "What is it?"

"Oh, nothing," she says half-heartedly. "I just... Well, I just got off the phone with Alice Forbes," she states, almost as if she's ripping off a Band-Aid.

My cheeks heat. She and my mother are close, the same with our fathers. Their friendly relationships are the reason why there's always been an understanding between Keegan and me, but it's not the reason why I care for him. I absolutely adore his mother. She's sweet and perky, and she never tries to look at my breasts when I'm having a conversation with her. Clearly, the bar is set low based upon personal experiences. "Is everything okay?" I ask.

She gives a trill laugh. "I'm warning you now, this conversation is going to be uncomfortable."

Oh, lovely. "Okay..."

I brace myself for what it is. Uncomfortable for my mother could mean a myriad of things. Is she going to tell me I looked fat in the pictures Eden posted of our trip? Is this some sort of womanly problem? The maid actually explained periods to me when I first got mine because Mother was too preoccupied with some fundraiser. Afterward, tampons just started showing up in my bathroom, and still to this day, I have no idea if my mother asked for them to be purchased, or if Gwendolyn did it herself.

Mom gives me a small smile as if she's already apologizing to me for what's about to come out of her mouth. I stare at the screen, riveted, and hoping that this isn't something bigger that Mom's downplaying like she always does. I mean, we're talking about a woman who doesn't care if her husband cheats on her. Maybe Dad had a heart attack, and this is how she wants to tell me.

"Keegan and Alice have some concerns about your relationship...with Keegan."

I sit up straighter, taken aback. Keegan's been my future. I've always known it. What's concerning me is her use of *concern* in that sentence in regard to my relationship with him.

"Keegan expressed worry that you might be a lesbian, and therefore, unable to commit to him in the future."

My mouth drops. A....lesbian? Is he for real right now? No wonder why I received those texts just before Mom called. "Because I wouldn't have sex with him?" I blurt.

She clears her throat. "That does seem to be the confusing part for the both of them, yes."

"Mom." My one-word protest is weak, but it's all I can muster at the moment.

I can't believe that freaking asshole went to his mother to complain that I wouldn't have sex with him. Even worse, that my own mother didn't just tell them to mind their own business and that I'll have sex with him in my own time. No, she has to call me up on the phone and ask if I prefer women.

At this point, I do.

"If you are, we'll work through it. We'll—"

"Mom," I interrupt her, but still nothing comes from my mouth. After several seconds go by, I exhale. "Really, Mom? This is what you're calling me about? I didn't realize that a relationship with Keegan would mean that my parents would get involved in it so personally."

"*I'm* being very sensible," she retorts. "I told Mrs. Forbes I didn't care if you were."

I guess that should make me happy? "But you're not even hearing yourself," I tell her, voice rising. "Just because I didn't have sex with Keegan, that makes me a lesbian?"

"I wasn't assuming, I was asking. This is just as embarrassing for me as it is for you."

"I'm not embarrassed," I spit. "I'm appalled that you didn't just tell them to mind their own damn business. If Keegan wants to know why I won't have sex with him, he can ask me. Also, he damn well knows why I won't have sex with him. He's just being...difficult."

"Language, Delilah," my mother reminds me.

I want to tell her "common sense" as my own rebuttal, but I clamp my jaw shut instead.

For several seconds, we just stare at each other until my mother gets fidgety. "Are you afraid? Sex is perfectly natural."

The more she talks, the more alarmed I get. "Are you seriously trying to talk me into having sex with him? You know, most mothers would be proud that their daughter is still a virgin."

Her eyes widen. She peers around the garden, most likely looking for an employee to have this conversation with me. Maybe the landscaper will do? Who knows what she's thinking. "Delilah, dear," she finally says. "It's great that you're this innocent, but

Keegan wants to explore this part of your relationship."

Relationship? We don't even have one at this point. I'm sitting here waiting for him to grow up. Is that too much to ask? I run my hands through my hair. "Does Dad know we're having this conversation?"

She huffs. "He told me to take care of it. Something about this being under my jurisdiction because you're a female and I'm a female."

Face heating, I ask, "So, he thinks I should have sex with Keegan too?"

She tilts her head in thought. "He didn't say, but I imagine since the Forbes are concerned that he is also."

I've heard a lot of interesting things while being amongst these powerful, rich people, but I'm not sure I've heard something this crazy. "Mother, I can assure you I'm not a lesbian. I can also assure you that Keegan knows why we're not having sex. You've just been used in some game Keegan's playing in which he thinks he can barter with my v-card or bully me into having sex with him. Please, if this comes up again, you can tell Mrs. Forbes to mind her own business."

My mother gasps. "I will do no such thing. Keegan is her business."

"Did Grandma ask you about your sexual status with Dad? Come on, this is ridiculous."

My mother leans toward the phone screen, gaze

narrowed. "I think you need to take a minute to calm down, Delilah Astor. Think about what you're doing and proceed ahead with all the knowledge you've received in that ridiculously expensive university you're attending."

Her finger moves toward the screen, and before I can come up with a cutting reply, she ends the video chat.

I blink at my phone, surprise still ricocheting through me. I have to hand it to Keegan, he knew how that would play out. He's no doubt laughing his ass off right at this moment. He knows me so well, it's easy for him to push every button that will set me off. My mother calling to ask about my sex life? Definitely a phone call to make me seethe.

Sure enough, as soon as my phone returns to the home screen, I find another text from Keegan waiting. **Two can play dirty.**

5

The bad thing about Carnegie is that everyone knows everyone.

I've been forced to play with the same kids my entire life. Growing up, we were all at the same vacation spots, and then in prep school, there we were again, all together. After all, there are only so many fancy places to send your children to school.

When I walk into the Campus Café the next morning, I almost wish I'd followed Eden to the West Coast. Forget about this following in my father's footsteps nonsense. If it means creating space between me and my intended, maybe I should pack my bags right now.

Keegan Forbes, in all his Carnegie University glory, sits on a leather couch. His cousin Devon, along with Anne-Marie Kennedy, are lounging with him in the comfortable seating area every classic coffee shop has. These velvet couches are flanked by house plants, leaves streaming down the front of black iron shelves in deep green waterfalls.

I nearly turn around and forget about the French vanilla cappuccino I've been craving, but he catches my eye before I can. He smirks, and I retaliate with one of my own before marching up to the counter to order my drink despite my skin crawling with the knowledge of what he tried to do last night.

He didn't send me another text after the one from yesterday, and I sure as hell didn't send him a response either. He thinks he's so clever going to our parents, like they can pry my legs open for him, but all I see is a whining, self-obsessed jerk.

After giving the barista my name, I breathe the deep-seated coffee aroma in and let it out before spinning on my heel and facing the problem head on. If I don't go over there, he'll just crow from his delusional perch of superiority. Since I can't let that happen, I make my way toward him. The café is full, a usual sight on Monday mornings at Carnegie. I smile at a few of my friends along the way, wondering if he expected me to drop my panties the next time I saw him. That's definitely not what's going to happen.

"Delilah, hi," Devon greets me. He stands, all six foot of him, and gives me a kiss on the cheek. Now here's a Forbes I like. Too bad his dad is the black sheep of the family. Devon's only attending CU because of the good graces of Keegan's father, proving that the Forbes men can actually be decent guys—when they want to be.

I reach up on my tiptoes to return the kiss. He's got the Forbes good looks and none of the pompous ways. Plus, he always smells good. Today, he could be a caramel apple sitting on a shelf at a bakery. I inhale on the sly and then step back. "So good to see you." I don't ask him how his break was. He only ever goes somewhere fun if Keegan's father decides to take pity on him, and since I know he wasn't on the Forbes' yacht, I keep my mouth shut, so he doesn't feel awkward. I take a seat next to him on the couch and smile at the girl next to Keegan. "Hi, Anne-Marie."

"Hey," she says breezily. Anne-Marie isn't my biggest fan, and I'm not hers either. She's hooked up with Keegan in the past. A fact she thinks I care about, but I don't. Her huge sunglasses are perched on top of her loose, raven black curls. Her tan is to die for. Even with the weather turning chilly, she's sporting a tank top with an off-the-shoulder cardigan, no doubt to show off her perfectly bronzed skin.

It takes me a while to gather the courage to look at Keegan. His golden-brown hair glints against the early morning sun streaming in through the window behind him. Blue eyes spark with mischief as he lets his gaze consume me. Before I can get swept away in remembering how he touched me, I turn my attention somewhere else, *anywhere* else.

Devon nearly spits out his coffee. "Frosty," he mumbles under his breath.

Devon and I have always been co-conspirators when it comes to Keegan. We both know he can be so much better than he is. We've seen it in him, it's just drawing it out that is proving to be the difficult part. Honestly, out of the entire Forbes family, Devon will be my favorite relative. Just to piss off Leon, I'll probably ask him to be in the wedding party. Won't he love seeing the black sheep of the Forbes clan in his precious son's nuptials?

It makes me grin just to think about it.

"How's Eden?"

Devon must envy her for going off and forging her own path. He's truly appreciative of CU and the other things the Forbes have deigned to give him, but he's always been more free-spirited than the rest of us here. He's more like Eden than me. Maybe that's why I like him so much. "She's—"

"She's going downhill," Keegan interjects. He sits forward, placing his elbows on his knees. "She's far too conceited."

I nearly snort. "Her? Conceited? I don't think you understand the meaning of the word, Keegan Forbes."

He prods me with a death glare. "When she thinks she's better than the best...that's conceited." I can only assume he's the best in this scenario. I turn to talk to Devon but Keegan can't keep quiet. "Here's another word I know the definition of." In true Forbes fashion, he leaves a pregnant pause, waiting until all of our eyes are on him. He scowls at me. "Prude. Prig. Goody two-shoes. Boring."

My back straightens. I meet his hard glare and then swing it to the other two. They're listening raptly, of course. Whatever problems Keegan and I have had in the past, we've kept it to ourselves. He must be past that now, bringing our parents into it and now this. "Good boy," I snark back. "I'll get you a thesaurus for Christmas so you can keep going."

"Excellent. I'll need synonyms for lesbian since my future wife swings that way."

"Keegan," I chastise, face heating. It's not about him erroneously calling me a lesbian, it's about him airing our dirty laundry in public.

"Dude," Devon interjects in my favor. "That's not cool." Anne-Marie just sits back and grins. I can practically see the wheels in her head turning. Keegan Forbes is a highly sought-after bachelor. That's why girls are always throwing themselves at him. He'll make any wife extremely happy in the monetary department, but it's never been about that for me.

"What's not cool…" Keegan continues. "…is Delilah Astor holding out on me. Still."

My heart races, and my throat starts to close, blocking any rebuttals that might spring to mind. I don't have confrontations, especially not with Keegan, especially not in front of other people. In our world, people remember shit. They lock it away for future use. One day, I might be in the same boardroom as Anne-Marie, and she's going to remember this very moment and wonder how she can use it to exploit me. I take in a deep breath, making sure my voice is calm when I speak. "I'm sure you can find someone else to scratch your itch, as you happily informed me of. Was it you, Anne-Marie?" It would make sense, actually, due to her amazing tan.

"Careful," she smirks. "Your jealousy is showing."

I can't hold back the laugh that rips from my throat. One thing I've never been jealous of is the way Keegan uses girls. I've carefully planned our relationship out. When we finally do get together, he's with me and only me. I won't even remember Anne-Marie's name. "Not a chance," I tell her.

Striking, hard blue eyes meet mine. Jaw clenched and shoulders stock still, he glares straight into my eyes. The tension between us thrums with electricity. "I've got another word." He dangles the carrot in the air like we're puppets waiting on his every word. "Virgin."

My ears ring, tuning everything out except for the very word that just came out of his mouth. I shift my gaze to Anne-Marie who has her hands over her mouth, round, stunned eyes crinkling at the corners, clearly betraying the fact that she's laughing.

"Keegan, what the fuck?" Devon barks. He places his coffee cup down on the table with a bang.

Keegan doesn't pay attention to him. He snickers after watching my reaction. Mortified doesn't even begin to cover it. Our world is built on secrecy, and he just took the most private part of me and laid it bare. What twenty-one-year-old is a virgin nowadays? Especially someone who—on the outside—has everything.

The worst part? I know for a fact that he loves that I'm a virgin. Why is he trying to use it against me?

"Thanks for inviting me for coffee, Keegan," Anne-Marie simpers. "This has been super entertaining."

She'll make me the laughingstock of the school now, which was probably his goal all along.

"Hey." Devon reaches over to squeeze my leg. "You okay?"

Behind me, a rough voice permeates the tension ping-ponging between the four of us. "French vanilla cappuccino?"

I turn. A guy in a stained barista apron stands in

front of me. Stubble dots his cheeks until it disappears into cocoa-colored hair that curls around the outer edges of a dark green cap. He looks like a local. Not to sound catty, but there's a difference. Everyone that attends school here looks like they ate caviar for breakfast, yet he looks down-to-earth and normal as he balances a white, ceramic cup on a matching saucer.

Instead of answering him, I turn to Keegan. "You know, glad you brought that up. I should take care of that, shouldn't I?" Standing abruptly, I inadvertently force the barista back with my drink order in his hands. I take it from him and set it down on the black coffee table at my back before facing him again. "You're good looking."

Burnt crimson highlights his cheeks. The same rough voice comes out. "Thank you."

"And...you look like you could help me out with a problem I'm having."

The guy squints, turning his head like he doesn't catch my meaning.

Of course he doesn't understand what I'm doing. What kind of crazy girl propositions their barista before their morning caffeine fix?

"Don't you dare," a dark voice threatens from behind me.

I don't know if Keegan is talking to me or my new friend, but I don't care. He wants to humiliate me, I can retaliate. After all, that's how business is done. "What's your name?" I ask my new friend, ignoring the male testosterone building behind me. If his hormones were a physical object, they would be a spiked battering ram aimed straight at me, I'm sure.

"She doesn't care," Keegan snaps.

The barista shifts his gaze over my shoulder, but I regain his attention by placing my hand on his jaw. His thick stubble tickles my palms. I'm an asshole for doing this, but I forge ahead because the embarrassment is all too real right now. I breathe out, making him look at me. "I actually do. I may go to this school, but I'm not a dick like everyone else."

The last comment was definitely for Keegan, and it must have hit my intended target because he comes up behind me, bringing his anger with him. Wrapping his arm through mine, he tugs me away. "What are you doing?" he growls.

"Keegan," I protest as I'm being dragged toward the café door like a child. He holds on tight, not giving me an inch of space. I can't stop us so I just go with it. Looking back, I watch as Devon talks the barista out of following me, and I make a note to apologize to him later. I shouldn't have brought him into it. "Keegan, let me go," I demand as we step outside.

He doesn't free me until we're on the opposite side

of the building. Forcing me against the stone wall, he leans in, seething. "What do you think you're doing?"

I lift my chin in the air. "What am *I* doing? You just told everyone I'm a virgin. That's private." The backside of my eyes heat. Tears pool in the corners. I'm desperate to erase what just happened. Call me an idealist, but I really was waiting for the perfect opportunity to share myself with Keegan, and here he's gone and thrown the one thing I kept sacred in my face.

"Everyone? Spare me the dramatics."

"You know Anne-Marie won't keep her mouth shut," I grind out. "It's why you did it. You want to humiliate me."

He licks his lips. Those same eyes that stared down at me with so much concern when he pulled me out of the water when I was four now stare down at me with an emotion so contrasting that it nearly takes my breath away. "What if I don't care if everyone knows? I'm staking *my* claim. Everyone is aware of our situation. They'll all realize you're saving yourself for me."

"Maybe I won't after this, Keegan." I'm exhausted. It shouldn't be this hard to be with someone. "You've taken it too far. You can't bully me into having sex with you."

"I don't need to bully you into doing anything. You want it, Dee. Tell me you haven't thought about my cock pumping inside that sweet pussy of yours."

I lock my jaw down, breathing through my nose. I wish I could take away all of my senses, but I can't. His dirty words, his dirty mouth, they make a pool of lava form in my belly, stretching out toward my core. He reads me too damn good to lie, too.

He grins. "I told you, Delilah." Leaning forward, his lips touch the shell of my ear. "You want me. Let me give you a good fuck to unwind all that stress inside you. That perfect, business-like, Barbie doll image you've got in your head. Let me make you scream it out."

His chest presses against mine. I breathe into him, my nipples brushing against his hard pecs. He shifts until his stomach is against mine too. The tease of his abs makes my brain go foggy, and I lose my breath when his erect cock comes next, bracing against his khakis as he rolls into me.

Before I lose myself in him, I push him back. He's a lot easier to take when he's glaring at me. I can form thoughts better. I can make more practical decisions. "I've been waiting for you to grow up for a long time," I tell him. "Don't go down this road, Keegan, or I will find someone else to lose my virginity to."

I push away, and he doesn't follow. My legs wobble as I make my escape, but I know that's not the end of it. It never is with Keegan Forbes. "What? Like with that loser in there?"

I peer over my shoulder. "If that loser wouldn't ever tell a whole group someone's virginal status, then yes. I'd take him any day over you."

The look of pure hatred that follows sends shivers down my spine.

My dad wasn't kidding when he said growing up with these kids was just like being involved in a hostile business takeover. You're either enemies, or your allies.

Keegan's supposed to be my number one ally, but I have no idea what happened.

6

After morning classes, where I spend my time staring at people I know and wondering if they're looking back at me because Anne-Marie couldn't keep her mouth shut, or if they're just, in general, looking at me, I drop back by the café. Not only did I get a bunch of homework dumped on me by professors who apparently missed their students too much, I'm pretty sure I've only been half functioning all day due to my run-in with Keegan.

While I wait in line, I check my social media to make sure Anne-Marie hasn't been doing something so dreadful as to post sneaky updates alluding to my status. Thankfully, her timeline has been quiet all morning. Her last post was of her lying in bed, dark hair fanned out over a silk pillow, telling the world she'll be back at CU in the morning.

The customer in front of me finishes ordering and steps out of the way. That same gruff voice sounds again, and I peer up, blinking. The barista from this morning waits to take my order. My cheeks heat so fast I'm sure he can see the embarrassment on them for himself. I slip my phone in my pocket and give him a timid smile. "Hi."

He blinks at me. "French vanilla cappuccino, right? I'll get you one on the house since you didn't get to drink yours this morning." He stares at me afterward as if he's waiting for me to acknowledge.

I give him a quick nod. "You don't have to do that though."

He shrugs, immediately turning to start making my drink. The other barista finishes with the previous customer and moves to the back. The speaker overhead plays a soft, languid tune. Looking around, I realize the place is mostly empty. It's just him, me, and the complicated coffee machinery.

Watching him work intrigues me. I've always found it fascinating to observe people while they're in their element. Gorging on hours of reality medical shows isn't abnormal for me, usually putting them on for background noise while I study. There's something so calm and reassuring about people who are good at what they do. It makes the world a little less chaotic.

He peers over his shoulder. "You can sit. I'll bring it to you."

I give him a smile as a thanks and then turn around. I have my pick of seats this afternoon. Avoiding the couches from this morning like the plague, I choose a high back armchair with a perfect view of the quad.

I barely have time to put my bag down before he's coming over with the café's signature, bright white coffee mug. He sets it on the small, circular table in front of me. Reaching for my bag, I say, "Are you sure I can't pay?"

He shakes his head. "Like I said, it's on the house." He shifts from foot to foot. "I was—" He clears his throat. "—sorry, I was thinking about you today. I know I don't know you, but I wanted to see if you were okay?" He ends the sentence like a question, as if he's unsure of himself.

It's a change of pace to see someone speaking without absolute authority. It's kind of nice, actually. His green hat is spun backward now, hair still curling out over the edges in an adorable way. I'm sure Keegan and I made quite the scene this morning. Any normal person would ask me if I'm okay since he basically dragged me from the café, but we're not always talking normalcy when we're in my world. "Yeah, sorry about that earlier. I'm fine, actually. Just..." I let the sentence stand on its own because I can't explain to this guy what happened. How embarrassing.

"Just a guy being a jerk? Your boyfriend?"

I wrap my hands around the huge mug, my thumb lightly moving over the warmed ceramic. "That's going to be an even longer story," I joke. "How much time do you have?"

He smirks, and a dimple appears in his cheeks. As men go to lose your virginity to, he looks like a great option. Not that I'm actually still contemplating that. I only said it to piss Keegan off, but of all the guys I could've picked, at least he's believable. "At the moment, not many since I'm on the clock."

I peer over at the counter. No one is in line yet, but the other worker is currently wiping down the flat surfaces, shoulders shifting with the overhead music. "Don't get in trouble on my account," I tell him. "I really am fine. Just a guy being a jerk. I can handle that."

He shifts his gaze down my body, hitting my toes before working his way slowly upward as if he's really trying to gauge whether or not I can handle myself. It's not an awkward feeling to have him size me up. It's nice. It's real. "My name's Tim, by the way."

I stand, reaching my free hand out. "Delilah. Thank you for helping me earlier."

He slips his coarse hand over mine, and I give him

a quick, firm handshake just like my father taught me. However, he doesn't let me go right away. It's only a fraction of a second, but it's enough to make me look him in the eyes before he smoothly releases my hand, making sure to drag his fingers over mine before fully releasing his hold. "Nice to meet you, Delilah. You should tell your friend that I don't take people like him treating women the way he did lightly."

His words vibrate around me, and I lower my gaze. "I will," I tell Tim, immediately regretful that I brought any more attention to myself and this screwed up scenario I have going on with Keegan. I definitely don't want him to get hurt. I just want him to grow up a little. "He's actually not that bad when you get to know him."

"If you say so," Tim says. He takes one look at me and walks away, moving beyond the swinging counter door where he starts up an easy conversation with the other worker. Both of them peer at me discreetly, so I must be the topic of discussion.

I finish my cappuccino hurriedly. I don't want to ask Tim for a to-go cup, but I also don't like being on display for people.

Just as soon as I've finished the last swallow, my phone vibrates. I take it out and stiffen when I realize it's a text from an unknown number. That, in and of itself, never used to get me, but it's also how the

Knights of Arcadia choose to communicate. Our next meeting to discuss upcoming events isn't supposed to be until Wednesday, but I'm being summoned now.

Despite what Tim said, I take a ten out of my wallet and throw it on the table before I make my way out of the café. He's not looking when I leave, so I don't bother with a goodbye.

Following the stone pathway to the center of campus, I then branch out to one of the most remote locations. Amidst a torrent of trees, a big, beautiful old building stands, maybe the most ornate at Carnegie. Which makes sense if you think about it. The Knights of Arcadia came before Carnegie. They're the reason the university even exists. They built this building promptly before erecting the others. Rumor has it that there's a myriad of tunnels underneath this building that connects to all the others on campus, and even some that lead into the surrounding forest.

As I approach the building, I receive another text. Pulling out my phone quickly, I realize it's a message from Keegan. I almost put my phone away again, but the preview of the picture he's sent me spurs my curiosity. I bring it up to fill the entire screen and stop in my tracks. He's sent a picture of me shaking Tim's hand at the café. When the phone buzzes in my hand again, another text from him comes in. **Don't test me, Delilah.**

Don't test him? Is he serious? I furiously type out a text. **Are you stalking me now??** After I hit Send, I shove my phone back in my pocket. What? Am I going to have to deal with this for the rest of my life?

Someone like Tim is sounding like the better option at the moment.

Instead of the building entrance being on the side that faces campus, it's actually on the complete opposite side where its only neighbors are trees. Peering around, I make sure no one is paying attention before I skate around the side of the building. I trail my fingers along the rough stone before arriving at the lion's head. A quick turn later, and a stone door releases, leaving just the barest of gaps. I press on the wall, grunting a little with the exertion, until the door swings freely. Once on the other side, I move it back into place where it's practically seamless. No one would know there was a door there if they weren't actively looking for it.

My stomach tumbles over itself when I'm met with a silent interior. Unlike the dorms where modernism has taken over, the Knights of Arcadia headquarters has kept its old-world charm. The walls are all rock. The floors have been refurbished, but gigantic, iron chandeliers along with ornate sconces still light the interior. The foyer reveals several tunnels that lead to different rooms. When I first became a fledgling Knight, overcoming all their obstacles, they gave us a tour that concluded in the basement where there are legit jail cells surrounding a giant pit in the middle of the space.

I take the tunnel to the left, moving toward the meeting room. I don't know who's called to meet me today or why. The hairs on my arms rise, goosebumps spreading toward my scalp. There are always elders around, lurking inside. We have some of the most prominent citizens of the United States in our ranks, so you never know who you're going to see. Except today, apparently. The building is quiet, as if it's holding its breath. The creep factor has increased one hundred percent. I've never been in it without other Knights around. The halls narrow. My deadening footsteps echo like a death knell.

Straightening my shoulders, I forge ahead. There's no one in the first meeting room. The second, though, is another story. I stick my head inside and freeze when I spot Keegan sitting in one of the fancy black leather office chairs. "Hey," I grind out, barging in. I'm about to tell him off for spying on me with Tim when movement at the head of the table grabs my attention. I stop where I am, shifting gears as Mr. Reginald Wright, one of the Knights on the board, sits.

Forcing a smile, I stare at the two of them. It's obvious Keegan is the reason why I'm being called in, and I have to drop the belief that this could just be a check-in to see how I'm doing. If Keegan is here, it isn't for anything good, especially since he's making me out to be his number one enemy lately. "It's nice to see you, Sir Reginald," I say, bowing.

"Miss Delilah, please have a seat." He gestures toward the leather chair opposite Keegan, and my heart skips a beat, wondering if my intended has now complained to the Knights that I'm not having sex with him. Why would they care though? No, that can't be it, but there are other ways that Keegan could get back at me.

With as steady feet as possible, I take my place at the table. Leaning forward, I place my forearms on the polished cherry table in front of me, facing down my tormentor.

"Thank you for coming so quickly," Sir Wright greets. "As you know, when one Knight—whether fledgling or not—makes a complaint against another, we believe in complete honesty."

I glare at Keegan, wondering what the hell he's doing. It was bad enough that I had to fight harder than any of the guys to be allowed in this space, now he's going to make it worse for me? "Yes, I'm aware," I say icily, hoping to strike Keegan Forbes down with my gaze. Right now, I can't find any remnants of the boy who saved me. The guy sitting across from me right now is a self-satisfied douche.

"Fledgling Forbes has expressed his concerns about your ability to fit in with the rest of the Knighthood." The elder gentleman, sporting salt and pepper hair, only takes a slight breath before forging on. "We knew there would be some getting used to with the first female amongst our midst, but you stated plainly that there wouldn't be any issues."

I remember that day, and he's right, I did state it plainly. I have—and had—no intention of anyone getting in my way of becoming a full-fledged Knight, even if I was the only one singled out with an extra interrogation to make sure I really was strong enough to be a Knight despite how I competed during the trials. "I did, Sir," I agree, lifting my chin and staring Keegan down.

He makes a low humming sound. "Why, then, do we find ourselves in this predicament with Keegan Forbes? Certainly, his father and yours have been friends for many years, so he is the last Knight I expected to make such a complaint against you."

He's right. He certainly should be the last. Keegan should be my everything and not the reason I'm now being spoken down to with such disdain with the accusation of falling back on my word. He's placed me into an impossible position. I doubt if I were to counter his claims that it would change Sir Reginald's feelings on the matter.

My gender has muted me. I don't have the liberty of speaking up and being heard, like Keegan has. I don't have the ability to lobby against Keegan's word because I'll be seen as difficult and not a team-player.

It's a sad realization to come to, only cemented when I glance at Sir Reginald who lifts his brows, waiting for me to speak.

Nausea and acid flip over in my stomach. I've spent my life trying to make sure I don't ever feel this way. I've worked my ass off to be the perfect daughter, the perfect student, the everything anyone would wish me to be. Except now, I'm thrown back in my "place."

It doesn't matter who you are, you can still get stuck. Still forced into a tiny hole because there's always someone bigger and stronger than you.

Right now, that person is Keegan for me, and he's making sure I know it.

7

Somewhere within the deep recesses of the Knights headquarters, water drips. It's overwhelming, the sound compounding as if it's counting down the seconds until I figure out the best way to answer Sir Reginald. He's basically asking me why Keegan has complained about me, placing the onus on my shoulders.

Straightening my shoulders, I breathe in deep and force a smile to my face before meeting Keegan's stare. He's forcing me to play nice, and I don't like it, but I have zero recourse. "I'm sorry Mr. Forbes feels that way. I'll endeavor to make better choices."

The thing about infiltrating a centuries old boys' club is that sometimes you have to swallow your pride and play their ridiculous games. I knew joining would be a rocky road, but the face staring back at me has gone beyond my own fears. Keegan should be the one person who's on my side. If he cared, he would be.

"I sure hope that's the case, Fledgling Astor. I know how proud your father is. You competed so well in the trials. I would hate to see our first female member not make it to graduation as a Knight."

His steady, carefully compiled words deaden my stomach. The threat is clear. What Keegan thinks of me matters. What the rest of the Knights think of me also matters. Their opinions will make a world of difference moving forward. Keegan was smart enough to understand that and is now exploiting me for it. He knows how furious I must be underneath this calm mask.

Constructing a response is difficult, but I do my best. "That would be a shame, but I'm sure it won't come to that."

Sir Reginald dribbles his fingers across the cherry wood. He shifts his scrutinizing stare from me to Keegan. "Acceptable, Fledgling Forbes?"

"Acceptable," Keegan says, smiling. As soon as Sir Reginald's attention fixes elsewhere, he mouths, *For now*. If I could give him an invisible dick punch, I would. He deserves it and more.

"Excellent, do keep me updated on the situation, Keegan." The elder gets to his feet, checking his watch. "I'm afraid I'm late to play squash with your father."

Keegan stands. "Give my father my best." He holds his hand out, and they shake as if co-conspirators. I swallow the bile inching its way up my throat in response.

Sir Reginald stops at my chair and places a hand on my shoulder. "You should join a planning committee, Delilah. Make friends. Network. The Devil's Night Party planning should be starting soon."

Devil's Night? Even though I've never heard of it, I nod at my assessor, making sure to give him a winning smile lest he think I'm a miserable bitch.

His footsteps echo around the chamber until he exits through the doorway. He takes some of the tension with him, but not all of it. Keegan grins, a purely evil sentiment because he doesn't realize what he's done. The weight of everything that just happened comes crashing down. Now that I don't have to pretend, I start sucking in air to calm myself. The idea of graduating as a Knight has never seemed so far away. It's as if I can see my goals toppling to the ground one-by-one. I blink before peering up at Keegan. "Why are you doing this to me?"

"You wanted to play games, I'm playing games."

"Is this about the guy at the café?" I ask incredulously, my fingers curling into my palms. Keegan rolls his eyes, squats to pick up his suede messenger bag, and starts to walk from the room. I scramble after him, whisper-shouting to him as we go. "It is, isn't it?"

"This has nothing to do with that loser," Keegan argues. "It has everything to do with you making me look like a fool though."

The tunnel opens up into the main chamber. The bulbs that they have in the chandelier make it look like the room is lit by real flames. Lights dance across the floor as I close the gap between us. "You mean after you called me a lesbian and told everyone I was a virgin?"

Keegan stops with his hand on the door release. "Everyone knows we're getting married one day. You made me look like an ass, Delilah. Hitting on some other guy in front of me. Implying that you were going to lose your virginity to *him*." He flicks the lever up, and the rock door swings toward us.

"Are you listening to yourself?" I practically screech once we're outside. "How many girls have you been with? How many have you paraded in front of me?"

"Paraded is an exaggeration."

I grip his sleeve, and he turns to face me. His blue eyes spark, and I nearly topple over from the force behind them. He's really angry for someone who acts like he doesn't care about me. "Just admit you made a dick move and I'll apologize for the barista stunt," I offer. I'm throwing him a major bone. None of what he just did to me inside the Knights headquarters is okay. Even if he does apologize, we're so far from being even. The part of me that's talking is the one that's always been in love with Keegan Forbes. This little piece inside of me knows there's a good guy lurking in there somewhere.

Keegan's brows pull together, the area between his eyes dimple with concentration lines. They smooth out barely a second later. "Can't do that, Dee. You crossed the line. You went so far over the line that you need to be punished."

He turns and walks away. I stare after him, slack-jawed for a few moments before I barrel after him. There's no way I can let him get away with that. "Is this about sex again? You're willing to dangle the Knights over my head because I won't have sex with you?"

He shrugs. "I never wanted you to join the KOA."

"So, what?" I'm hot on his heels as he makes his way around the building and strides across the stone pavers. Fallen leaves dot our path, crunching underneath our solid footsteps. "So, because you never wanted me to, that means I shouldn't? You don't get to make all the decisions, Keegan. This is what I'm talking about when it comes to you. It's my right as an Astor to be a Knight. I worked hard. I made it. You don't get a say."

Before I know it, Keegan's taking stone steps two at a time. Glancing up, I realize we're at my dorm. He enters the front door like he owns the place and continues up the stairs where he stops at my door.

I block it, fanning my hands out and clutching the frame. "What are you doing? You're not going in there."

His eyes gleam from the challenge. "You'll let me in, or I'll start telling every single one of your house mates that you're a virgin. Maybe I'll even drag one of them out here and fuck them while you watch."

I glare at him and his cut, muscled chest. He's not just going to leave, and he'll probably do one or both of what he just threatened me with. Since I don't want our business broadcasted, I turn my back, fish my keys out of my bag, and open the door.

Upon entering, Keegan drops his messenger bag on the floor. The thwack it makes against the wood planks raises the hair on my neck as I place my own bag gently down on my desk. "I never wanted you to be a Knight because that's not how things are supposed to be, Delilah. I'm the man. I'm supposed to go to CU. I'm supposed to graduate with honors as a Knight. I get the good job, running my father's company, providing for my wife," he bites out, voice eerily calm, even though I detest the sentences he strings together. "I don't want my wife competing with me for every damn thing. I can't even be a man around you. You won't let me perform my basic duties," he snarls while greedily taking in my body. Taut muscles, tense enough to theoretically snap at any moment, tighten even further.

"You think I'm emasculating you?" My mouth drops the longer I think about it. He totally does. This actually makes sense. It's totally Keegan's MO, and I'm not sure why I never put it together before. "Keegan, I'm—"

"Stop," he demands, lifting his hand. "I know you're about to spout some feminist bullshit at me. I get that you want to be your own person, but there are some things that are sacred."

"Like the Knights?"

"Like the Knights," he seethes.

I don't even know what to do with that. These are exactly the types of opinions I'm trying to change. Backing down isn't an option for me. "You've always known I wanted to work. Dad's expecting me to take over his hospitality businesses. I *want* to."

He starts forward, and I step to escape him until the backside of my knees hit the bed. I sit ungracefully, and he towers over me. "You know what I want? My wife to be waiting for me when I get home from a long day's work. Maybe in a sexy, silk robe. Maybe in absolutely nothing. I want to be buried inside her so deeply that I forget all about the tedious shit I had to do that day. I can't do that if my wife is still at the office."

My tongue sticks to the roof of my mouth. I breathe in, chest heaving. He smells like expensive cologne, the kind he used to steal from his father's walk-in closet so he could pretend he was grown. He's not a little kid anymore, though, and the scent wafting off him is an aphrodisiac to my traitorous body, surrounding me in a lust-filled haze. My heart beats in my chest, a rhythm that is in stark contrast to my head. Keegan's allure undermines me, but I can't help falling for it every time. "Maybe we'll fuck the tedious shit out of each other when I get home," I tell him, hopeful.

"Says the girl who won't let me touch her."

"Do you want to know why, Keegan? Have you bothered to ask yourself that question? You keep telling me that I want to, and you're obviously right. But once I let you go there, you're going to have the power to break me—more than you already do."

"Give in," he growls, placing his hands on the bed on either side of my hips.

He forces me back. Placing one knee on the mattress, he begins to crawl over me. I clamp my knees to his hips, trying to stop him from going any further. "You give in," I urge. "You know what I want. You can read me so well, you always could. Don't play dumb when it comes to this just because you're thinking with your dick."

He drops his gaze to my chest, zeroing in on the slight peek of cleavage poking through the scooped neck of my shirt. He lowers his stare until he places his palms on my knees and forces them to the bed. I'm wearing jeans, but I still feel exposed as he focuses on my inseam. Drifting his hands inward, he curves his palms over my thighs until he rubs his thumb in circular motions directly over my clit. How he pinpointed that exact spot through my jeans is beyond me.

"Keegan," I warn, but my frail attempt has less to do with him and more to do with me. I should be shouting my own name, alerting myself to the major screw-up that's about to happen, but I don't want him to see my weakness. The truth is, I like the picture he painted of our marriage. Me, laid out on the bed, counting down the minutes until he walks in with his sexy suit and tie. Or me, waiting for him with my bikini on in the hot tub. I can see it all, just as picture perfect as he made it sound.

"Give in," he breathes.

"Do you want me?" I squeak out, telling myself not to focus on the way my body responds to him. "Not sex. *Just* me."

"They go hand-in-hand, Dee."

I shake my head as he quickens his tight circles over my clit. He has to press hard to get me to feel it through the thick material of my jeans, and it scares me a little that he knows the right amount of pressure. "You know I've always wanted you," I plead, attempting to elicit a response from him. I told him the same thing the night I found out he cheated on me. Sobbing, I called him up to reveal my biggest secret: I've loved him ever since he saved my life.

He said nothing at the time. The line went mute. After a minute with no response, I hung up the phone. It didn't stop my tears from coming. In fact, it only made them worse.

I meant it when I told Tim that the story between Keegan and me was a long one. It's filled with cracks and potholes, barely ever a smooth surface in sight.

He reaches for my zipper, and I don't stop him. Maybe I want to pretend that he could be good for me. Just this once. His fingers curl around the top of my jeans, and he pulls them down past my ass and thighs.

His pupils are huge as he takes in my damp panties. He runs his fingers along the edge, flirting with the lace. "You're so wet for me." My clit is begging for more attention, and I have no doubt I dampen my panties further just as he watches and waits.

"What are you doing to me, Delilah? I should be

off nutting with some other girl who'll actually let me fuck her right now."

"Why don't you just take it?" I ask. He already knows I clearly want it, but yet, he hasn't taken it that far. It's the one saving grace I've been leaning on when I think there's no good parts left in Keegan.

"Because I want to make you beg for it." The hope I've built up squashes. The Keegan staring back at me is sinister and dark. "Not until you're on your knees, pleading for me to fuck you will I ever enter your pretty little cunt."

If I was expecting poetry, I was dead wrong. Of course Keegan would be wanting me in some way that humiliates me, not builds me up. I swallow, tasting the wrongness of his words on my tongue. "You'll have to wait a long time."

He reaches out, grips my panties, and shreds them into two. The unexpected cool air caresses my sensitive flesh, and my pussy clenches. "Not as long as you think," Keegan smirks.

When his hands reach toward my core, I think it's because he's going to play with me again, sink his finger inside me. He doesn't. Instead, he spreads my folds and bends over to lick up my pussy. My hips jump off the bed. "Keegan." It's too intimate. It's too far. My mind yells these two things at me as my body has other ideas.

It searches his tongue out, following him as he ravishes my core.

My fingers curl into my sheets. I brace myself, trying to get my mind and body on the same page, but my mind eventually gives in to my impulses. It's as if I don't care that he completely humiliated me in front of a Knight elder a little while ago. Or I've forgiven him for the virgin stunt he pulled this morning in front of the biggest gossip at Carnegie. Or I've completely forgotten about the fact that he just told me he doesn't want the type of wife that I want to be. It's as if my mind doesn't catch up to the fact that we're completely wrong for each other when he's making my body feel the opposite.

Keegan pauses, gingerly drifting his lips across my sensitive flesh. "Tell me it feels good."

I clamp my jaw shut, but my breath still ravages in and out.

"Dee..."

"My breathing isn't evidence enough?" I snap, waiting for him to start again.

"No, not nearly," he says. "Tell me, and I'll finish you off. Tell me how damn good I'm making you feel."

To prove his point, he backs away a smidge. On alert, my brain tells me this is just part of his mind game, but fuck, I'm so close to the edge. I need the release. He can't back away now. That's the last thing I want. While I war within myself, he blows a hot breath over my core. I break. The sensations are just too overwhelming. "Fuck, it feels so good."

Keegan moans deep in his throat. "You swear when you're horny. Keep going."

My skin bristles. "You keep going." He pinches my hip, and a yelp escapes my throat. I glare at him, but once he has my attention, he flicks his tongue across my clit. My hips immediately reach to meet his mouth. Hot pleasure swirls in my core. "Yes, Keegan. Please." He gives me a self-satisfied grin that twists my stomach. Instead of peering into eyes that tell me he knew he would win, I move my stare to the ceiling and focus on the complete bliss coursing through my limbs. He settles into a rhythm that barrels through me, the tip of his tongue circling my clit. My toes curl. "Yes, like that. God, it feels so good. More."

The more I talk, the more Keegan gets into it. He yanks me forward and sucks on my clit like a man starved.

"Jesus...fuck!" I cry out as my orgasm hits. He sucks and sucks, and my body responds with a climax like no other. My body shakes. My pussy clenches rapidly. "Keegan!"

The post-orgasm high is a state of euphoria. It takes minutes for me to calm down, my muscles relaxing once more. Eventually, Keegan clears his throat. I peer up at him, cheeks heating at the smug grin on his face. "Like I said, sooner than you think."

My heart constricts. It's clear there's a physical connection between us, but is there more? I don't think I can ever live up to his ideal. "Keegan, I can't be who you want me to be."

"Neither can I, Dee. Neither can I."

For the first time, sorrow blankets his features. Instead of talking it out, he spins, grabs his bag, and exits, leaving me there to pick up the pieces.

ater that night, I spend time Googling why I let someone like Keegan do this to me—even crave it—when I know I shouldn't. When I know he'll just turn around and be a jerk to me at some point in the very near future. I'll end up wallowing, asking myself every time: Why?

The all-knowing internet tells me it's just science. He's triggering my pleasure stimulus, so of course I want him to keep going, to bring me to climax no matter the consequences.

After reality sets in, though, the rational part of my brain takes over. Keegan's trying to get me kicked out of the Knights. He never wanted me to be one in the first place because I somehow threaten his manhood by taking control of my own life.

I'm not going to be his arm candy for the rest of my

life. I won't be able to live with myself when he starts cheating and I have to pretend I don't see, hear, or know anything. Sounds like the best way to slowly decay inside.

These thoughts spin through my head all through the night. I have a nightmare in which I'm Keegan's date at a future work function. No one talks to me. No one even looks at me. They laugh and joke, but I stand mute at Keegan's side. No matter how many times I try to open my mouth to join in on the conversation, something stops me every time. Eventually, I run away. Scrambling through a maze of halls, I frantically search for a mirror. When I finally find one, my lips are stitched together.

I wake with my heart beating like crazy as if it's trapped in my chest. I refuse to let this be my future, for Keegan to paint me into a box that I have to stay in. Before I even get out of bed, I send him a text, **We should talk.**

Afterward, I take my shower, brush my teeth, and dress for the day. I was too focused on Keegan last night to get any homework done, so I fill my bag with books and head to the library to get some studying done before my first class.

The stone structure that houses the library is the most modern on campus. It's been remodeled several times as the years have gone on, but there's still some historical parts. Once inside, I take the stairs to the study area where wood beams span the entire ceiling. The arched windows let in a lot of light, streaming through onto the carpeted floor that's the color of a deep, red wine.

"Psst."

I glance toward the sound of the noise and find Devon. I wave to him and walk over. At this time of day, there aren't a lot of people around, but we whisper anyway because of the way sounds carry in this building, especially so close to the rafters like this.

I set my bag down on his study table and sit opposite him. He peers up at me. "I was going to text you this morning. Are you okay?"

I take a deep breath and let it out. No matter how much I try not to think about Keegan's tongue on me, I can't seem to get it out of my head. I can't talk about that with his cousin though, so I lie. "Yeah. I'm good."

He narrows his gaze and calls me out. "Liar. Something else happened, didn't it?"

I swallow down my trepidation. It'll be good to get this out. I can't talk to my parents. Obviously. And Eden won't understand why I can't let Keegan go. She's always hated him. "Oh, just your cousin trying to ruin my life," I deadpan, smiling at him afterward to soften the blow. Not that Devon cares. He and I are on the same page with Keegan.

He shakes his head. "I've never met two people who were both simultaneously so right for each other and yet, so, so wrong. I think you might actually end up killing him."

I half snort. "I think it's the opposite. He takes delight in being mean to me."

"Not just you," Devon points out. "Listen, I know he was all pissed yesterday because Anne-Marie sent him a photo of you and the guy at the café shaking hands. Like that's some sort of crime. Did he do something else?"

I blink, recoiling slightly at this new information. "Anne-Marie sent him the photo? I thought he took it." Honestly, the timeline makes more sense if he didn't. He was most likely already having a chat with Sir Reginald when Anne-Marie snapped that picture of me and Tim.

"Yeah, I don't know if you've noticed, but she's basically all over your man."

I shrug. If he's going to let her be all over him, she can have him. I unzip my bag, take out a giant textbook, and open it. "Oh well."

Devon reaches out, placing his hand on my book so I can't turn the page. "Since I have the benefit of being a male, may I suggest to you that you're not doing yourself any favors when it comes to how Keegan acts around other women?"

I follow the line of his hand upward, past his shoulder, until I meet Devon's gaze. He's giving me a half-pitiful expression that makes me cock my head. "What?"

"Remember that we're not dealing with a normal guy here, okay? We're dealing with a Forbes. I'm excluding myself from what I'm about to say, of course. Forbes men are used to getting anything and everything they want. He sees you not even trying. He sees you not paying him any attention. He sees you not fawning all over him like you're in heat. *He* thinks you don't care." Pausing for a moment, he lets that sink in. "Now, you, being the intelligent one, is thinking, 'Hey, if he doesn't want me and only me—'"

I sit back in my wooden chair. "—then why would I fawn all over him?"

"Exactly." Devon grins like he just solved the world's problems.

I roll my eyes. "He told me yesterday that he can't be the person I want him to be."

"Not *can't*," Devon interjects. "*Won't*. He doesn't realize he can be different right now. You have more faith in him than he does."

I take a moment to ponder everything he's just said. I've always been the person who saw the best in Keegan, but what he did to me with the Knights is inexcusable. "He did something evil to me yesterday," I say cryptically. Devon knows about the Knights because he's a Forbes, but it's still a secret group. Outsiders aren't privy to what happens on the inside.

"Does this have something to do with the fact that he returned to his room in the afternoon and spent the next two hours in his room with the radio blaring? That usually only means one thing. Either he's got a girl in there, or he's..." He trails off but lifts his hand in the air, wiggling his fingers at me.

My mouth drops. I shouldn't be surprised that Keegan went back to his room to rub one out but I am. Why hasn't he even asked me to reciprocate? "There was probably a girl in there," I tell him, shrugging.

"Except there wasn't," Devon shares. "I borrowed one of his shirts, and I just happened to return it a few minutes before he got back. There wasn't anyone else in the room, and he was a miserable prick for the rest of the night. He said he had an incident at the—" Devon peers around the room and lowers his voice even further. "The Knights."

My stomach clenches, but Devon understands the need for secrecy as well as I do.

"You can tell me, Delilah," he urges. "Hell, I was on the Knights shortlist, but since dear old Uncle Leon wanted his son to be exclusive, I never made it." He shifts his gaze away, jaw ticking.

"It was a self-induced incident," I tell Devon,

hoping to take his mind off how unjust our world can be. "He put in a complaint against me."

Devon recoils. "Seriously? That's low."

"Yeah, I'm serious. He told one of the elders that I wasn't fitting in. Of course, being the only girl, they expected it, so they didn't even try to hear both sides. There was nothing I could say."

Devon leans back and runs his hand through his hair. "That's shitty, for even him. He knows how much you wanted it."

"He doesn't think I should be a Knight either, apparently," I grouse, still hurt by his words from yesterday. We have two very different visions for our future, that's for sure. I brush imaginary lint from my pants and sit up straighter. "Now, I have to be on my best behavior, a model Knight, including joining some upcoming planning committee like Devil's Night or something."

"Devil's Night?" Devon's eyes round.

"Yeah. You ever heard of it?"

"Well, yeah, but you're asking two different things. Regular Devil's Night is the night before Halloween where people play pranks on each other. Mischief, that kind of thing. But if you're talking Devil's Night for the Knights, that's a whole different scenario." He shakes his head. "It's mischief, alright, but in the debauched kind of way. Honestly, you're going to hate it. It's everything about our world that you despise."

I slump back in my chair. *Wonderful. Just what I need.* Letting out a breath, I prepare myself for the answer to my next question. "How do you know about it?"

Devon dribbles his fingers over the table between us. "When we were kids, Keegan and I followed his father to the party. We knew he was going to Dark Island, so we rowed there and hid in the shadows. The Knights own the castle there. It's been in the Knights' possession since it was built, and it's also where the Devil's Night Party is always held, but shh, it's a secret," Devon reminds me, pursing his lips together. "We were too young to see some of the things going on there. We didn't stay long because I begged Keegan to return home. The next year, Keegan snuck out by himself to watch from the wings. I'm pretty sure he's been waiting to go to his own Devil's Night for a very long time."

"Wha—What kind of things did you see there?"

"Think naked girls. Overindulgence. Sex."

The mantra of the old money I grew up around is *Work hard, play hard.* I'm not sure any of these men ever give that up. They have no stopping point, no moral compass. I can just imagine the things that go on at this so-called party.

By joining the Knights, I'd hoped to change some of that thinking. I suppose I can help by making sure I'm on the Devil's Night planning committee. Maybe tone the party down. However, I'm already on Keegan's shit list. If he thinks I'm out to change the night he's looked forward to for a long time, he'll retaliate in even more extreme ways.

I groan, and Devon grins. "Sorry to be the bearer of bad news. I'd help you, if you know, I was actually allowed to be a Knight."

Sympathy swamps over me. I've never liked how Devon gets treated just because his dad and Keegan's don't get along. "That's ridiculous, and I'm sorry, Devon. If it were up to me, I'd have put you in the running."

He gives me a winning smile. "That's why you're my favorite rich person, Dee. Okay, wait, you're my second favorite rich person. You know Eden's my number one."

If I wasn't suspicious that Devon swung the other way, I'd have already dreamed of him marrying my sister. "You should call her," I tell him. "She'd love to hear from you."

"I've been trying to find a spare moment to do anything," he complains. "They've already started in with the heavy coursework." He gestures toward the open textbook in front of him. "I'm drowning in this stupid text."

Before I can commiserate with him, we're interrupted. "Hey, Delilah."

I peer toward our visitor and have to force a smile to my face when my gaze meets Cameron Cabot. He and Keegan used to be best friends. I've never liked him all that much. "Hey."

He leans on the table, the heel of his palm gripping the edge. He gives me his cheesy smile, the one he thinks every girl loves. I'm about to ask him if he feels okay when he tiptoes his fingers across the table and onto my textbook. I briefly peer up at Devon with a "what the fuck" expression. He shrugs. "So..." Cameron starts. "I saw you over here and just wanted to come by and say that I can help you with your problem, if you want."

I tilt my head. I have zero clue as to what he's talking about. Briefly, I check the textbook to see if I brought out Physics. When there's nothing on the page but text, I peer back up at him. "Problem?"

He bends his knees to lower himself eye-to-eye with me. "You know, being a virgin?" he whispers. "That's something I can definitely help with."

My face blazes with heat. The way he rakes his gaze over me makes my fingers shake. I dig them into my textbook and glare back at Cameron. "Thanks for the offer, but I'm actually fine. No problem at all."

"If Keegan can't seal the deal, I thought maybe you'd want to look elsewhere." He leans closer, reaching his hand toward my shoulder. "I've had virgin pussy before. I'll make it nice for you, Delilah. I'll go easy."

I stand straight up. The need to get away from him is just too much. The force tumbles my chair over, hitting the carpet with a thud. "Dude, lay off," Devon snaps.

I suck in a breath, trying to calm the erratic beat of my heart. With a quick tug on my clothes to make sure they're all nicely arranged, I say, "No, it's fine. Here's the thing, Cameron. I wouldn't let you touch me even if it meant I had to be a virgin for the rest of my life."

His face sours. "I was only trying to help."

"I fail to see the aid I need in getting laid."

"Well, apparently you do because Keegan will fuck anything. Except not you. You must be an icy bitch like he says."

He spins and leaves, and I glare after him. Is that what everyone thinks? Is Keegan telling everyone I'm like that? Devon starts to go after Cameron, but I reach out to grab his sleeve. "He's not worth it."

"I'm not going after that asshat, I'm going to tell

Keegan this little game he's playing with you is out of line."

I shake my head. "I'm fine."

"This time," Devon states. "You're fine *this time*. What happens when someone won't take no for an answer? Keegan's set you up to be the shiny gold piece everyone wants, and we both know there are a bunch of entitled dicks walking around this campus. They'll convince themselves you wanted it."

A shiver runs up my spine. Downstairs, the door bangs open, and I can imagine Cameron bitching to everyone who will listen about what just happened. Even if only a small number of people knew before, they'll all know now.

Shit just got way worse.

9

Devon follows me out of the library. So much for studying first thing this morning. Now I have an old boys' club to bring into the twenty-first century, rumors going around that I'm a virgin, and the guy-I'm-supposed-to-marry committed to making me beg for sex.

I'm walking fast, but Devon jogs ahead of me. I take a breath of relief, hoping he'll calm down, until he starts shouting, "Keegan! Hey, Keeg!"

I freeze where I am. Glancing around, I find Keegan walking across campus with a beautiful brunette. He glances at Devon and me and keeps going. Devon's like a dog with a bone though. He doesn't stop.

"Keeg, what the fuck? I need to talk to you."

Keegan gives the girl an apologetic smile, the likes

of which I haven't seen since we were in our early teens and tells her he'll hook back up with her later. When he finally turns to us, after checking the girl's ass out, he hikes his bag up his shoulder, looking bored. "What?"

"What?" Devon exclaims, thrusting his arm out at me. "Cameron Cabot just hit on your girl."

Keegan glares at me and snorts. "So?"

"So? So, he told her he could take care of her virginity problem, Keeg. You just made her the sweetest target among your simpering, selfish friends who are only looking to get their dick wet and the entitlement to believe they can get it anywhere."

Keegan's face turns an alarming shade of red. "They wouldn't touch her," he grunts, but he looks unsure. It's his uncertain face that makes the weight of all this settle on my shoulders. It makes me second guess the morality of some of these guys I go to school with. I'm sure I only know a small subsection of vulgar stories and games when it comes to the rich families of the world. Murder, love triangles. I haven't yet heard of virginity used as a game, but there's a time and a place for everything.

Devon levels his cousin with a glare. "You know that's not true."

"I'll kill him if he touches her. End of story." He turns his angry eyes to me. "And don't go thinking that you can use this as an opportunity to give that virgin pussy to someone else. It's *mine*." He steps so close his hot breath hits my cheeks. "Do you understand, Delilah?"

"Fuck off," Devon growls. "This is bigger than that."

The nerve of this guy. He's talking to me like I'm the one who started this. *He* told the biggest gossip at school I was still a virgin. Pushing past him, I force my shoulder against his to make him move out of my way. It works, but only for a short time. He runs next to me, and I shoot him a look. "What are you doing?"

"Walking you to class, making sure everyone knows you're mine."

"Keegan, you've got some nerve."

"Nerve to what?" He reaches over, placing a strand of hair behind my ear. It's an affectionate gesture that seems so wrong on him, especially at this moment. "Nerve to treat you like you're my future wife?"

"You told me just yesterday that you can't be who I want. Hell, you were just walking some other girl to class."

"You told me the same." I peek at him, and his eyes flash in dark shadows. "Dee, I'm not playing around. You're promised to me. You've *been* promised to me. I'm collecting, and there's no other way about it." He loops his arm through mine, forcefully, leading me toward the building that houses my first class. Honestly, I'm surprised he even knows where it is. The fact that he's even paid attention one iota is shocking. He takes me right to the door of my class and leans in toward me. "You might want to think about giving it up sooner rather than later. Everyone will leave you alone if you do."

I peer up at him through my lashes, wondering if this is all part of his plan. He'd know I'd hate it that guys were propositioning me for sex. "Start putting in the work."

He snickers. "What work? You already want my cock so far inside you that you can barely stand it. What was that last night? 'More, Keegan. Yes. More.'" He breathes heavily into my ear, and my cheeks warm. It's not embarrassment like it should be. It's excitement. A buildup of lust. He's turned me on right before I have to go to one of my hardest classes. He brushes his lips over my cheek. "Also, the first Devil's Night planning committee meeting is tonight. I'll text you the details."

When he leaves, it's almost as if the rational part of my brain gets vacuumed back into my body. I nearly stumble as he makes his way back down the hall and out the front doors. I enter class with a hollow chest and a mind that's on anything but this boring lecture.

The professor gives us yet another bevy of homework, and I walk from the room with my head down, hoping I'll go unnoticed. Someone falls in step alongside me though. I peek out of the corner of my eye and blow out a breath when I see who it is. "What do you want, Anne-Marie?"

Her answering laugh is the tinkling kind that sounds suspiciously like annoying bells. "I bet Keegan didn't foresee this. Half the seniors are taking bets they'll be the first to defile you."

My stomach clenches. "Ew."

"I loathe to agree with you, but I do."

"You loathe to agree with me, and yet, I wonder how all those people found out that I'm a virgin?"

"You're not kidding yourself, are you, Delilah? You're too smart for that. You absolutely have figured out that Keegan invited me to the café because he knew you'd be there. He knew he was going to drop some major truths that I would take and run with. Though, I think the virgin bit was an accident on his part. I'm sure he intended me to start the rumor about you being a lesbian because he thought it would humiliate you and prompt a frantic phone call from your parents."

"And yet, you let him get away with it," I accuse.

She gives me a winning smile, the same one I imagine she would give after just forcibly taking over someone else's business. "You ever realize that what we're living now is really just a precursor to what's ahead of us in the real world?" she muses. "Wake up, Delilah. You're in the pre-game already. People are out to slit each other's throats. If they can get rid of the competition now, that's one less they'll have to manage when we make it to the big time."

I swallow the lump in my throat. As soon as we step outside, she lowers the sunglasses over her eyes that were perched on her head and then swings her hair over her shoulder. I watch her walk away and know she's right. We've all been jockeying for position since we were kids. It just gets more dangerous every year. Now, we're not fighting over sand shovels and toys, we're lobbying with truths and mistakes. What happens in my social stratosphere, stays in my social stratosphere. For good.

I'll forever be known as the twenty-one-year-old virgin. I'll be laughed at during dinner parties and soirees. Hell, one day, I'll be holding my child's hand and someone will say, 'Remember when Delilah Forbes was a virgin at CU? Pathetic.'

Secrets are paramount in this social circle, and Keegan betrayed my trust.

If he thinks I'm going to slink underground, he doesn't know me at all.

I turn my phone on and weed through several different texts from guys who've known me my whole life who are now just suddenly interested in me. Briefly, I scan through their messages. Some are hiding their ulterior motives well. Others are blatantly coming out and saying exactly what Cameron Cabot did. They want to take care of my *problem*.

The thing is, I've never seen my virginity as a problem. It's a tool.

After getting the details about the committee from Keegan's text, I start across campus, mind reeling. My virgin status is kept there for a reason. I could easily give in. Hell, I could text one of these guys back right now and have them meet me at my room in ten minutes. I could've had sex with Keegan on the yacht and about a dozen other times in my life, but I didn't. I didn't because I knew that as soon as I did give it up to Keegan—and let's get real, it's always been Keegan—that he would believe he had me by the lady balls. Like his dick is so magical that I would fall in line with everything he wanted. Maybe I'm a little scared of that happening, too, if I'm honest.

For me, my virginity is a weapon to use against him. My last saving grace to get him to show the kind of man that I know he can be. And even if all that fails, it's something I have that I can be proud that I never gave up just because of our past. Keegan has to earn his spot between my legs, no matter if he does give me mind-blowing orgasms.

I rush behind the building that houses the café, heading for my room so I can prepare for the Knights committee meeting in a couple of hours. I do a double take when I spot Tim leaning against the side of the building next to the air conditioning unit. He wipes his forehead and crosses his arms, but that's not what's got my attention. He has a bandage over his forehead.

Changing course, I walk that way. "Tim?"

He peers up at me, eyes rounding briefly. He wipes his hands off on his apron. "Delilah, hey."

"What happened to you?" I ask, gesturing toward the white bandage.

His gaze lowers. "I got jumped."

I rear back. "Jumped? Here? On campus?"

"I was getting off work and walking home. I don't have a car," he explains. "These guys jumped out of the bushes near the main entrance."

Horror strikes me. I can't imagine something like that happening here. "I'm so sorry. Are you okay?"

His jaw tenses, and he shakes his head. "Just scraped up. I don't understand how you can go to school with these fucking punks. They're all self-centered assholes."

I blink, confused. He thinks it was one of the students here at Carnegie. They don't seem like they'd want to get dirty enough to rough someone up. They might pay someone else to do it though. I sigh. "Yeah, tell me about it." Walking closer, I take the spot next to him. From this vantage point, you can see a fair bit of campus. I imagine Carnegie University through his eyes. A bunch of posh, rich snobs who've gotten everything handed to them. I don't know what it is about Tim that makes me want to open up, but I do. Maybe it's because I don't want him to think he's the only one who has problems. "If you haven't heard, I'm a virgin, which, suddenly, somehow, makes me extremely attractive." He turns toward me, mouth agape. He looks so shocked that I laugh. "What? It's not that bad."

He shakes his head. "No, that's not it. Those fuckers were talking about you, and I didn't even realize it."

"What? What...fuckers?"

"Some douchebags talking about bagging a virgin. There was big money on the line for whoever was able to do it."

My stomach roils, and I peer away. "It's pretty sick, isn't it? I've known most of these guys my whole life, but I'm suddenly interesting. What about a girl who hasn't had sex before is attractive? I'll probably be terrible at it. You'd think they'd want someone with experience."

Tim clears his throat nervously. "No offense, but I don't think it's about you at all. It's probably just about ticking another box on their to-do list. If you really like a girl, it doesn't matter what her, you know, status is." His cheeks redden.

I press my lips together to hold back a laugh. "I made this conversation super awkward, didn't I? Sorry about that."

"Please, I'm pretty sure I called all of your friends stuck up assholes as soon as you showed up."

"Obviously, they're not my friends," I tell him, letting that thought sit on my shoulders like a ten-ton weight. We're all competitors, just like Anne-Marie said. When I started listening to her, I don't know, but she does have a point. "Ugh," I groan. "What a mess."

Tim turns toward me. "You know, whoever told everyone that you're a virgin probably isn't worth your time worrying about. I've only spoken to you a handful of times and I can tell that you're infinitely a better person than the rest of these guys. For one, you remem-bered my name and don't just call me Coffee Guy or Hey you."

"Well, I apologize on behalf of all these...fuckers," I tell him.

He chuckles at my use of the word, probably because it sounds awkward coming out of my mouth. If I think it sounds awkward, I'm sure others think so too.

Now that I think about it. Maybe he's right. Maybe someone did jump him just because he's not one of us.

"You should be careful out there, Tim. They're all predators."

"You, too, Delilah. See you around?"

I give him a smile and a wave before leaving. It's refreshing to talk to someone who doesn't think they're the best thing God put on this earth.

Honestly, Tim gives me a little more faith about the people in this world.

10

In between classes and the Devil's Night Party meeting, I study my butt off. As the time nears, the more my stomach clenches. Though a lot of our traditions as Knights are old school, participating in committees and joining together for task forces are a modern sentiment. Today, the Knights of Arcadia is run more like a well-oiled business than a fraternity club. The idea being that, as a whole, members can make each other better. Of course, when I say better, I mean richer, furthering the divide between the mega rich and the only moderately wealthy. One Knight is even funding the first commercial spaceship to Mars. Talk about mind blown.

My nerves are as tight as taut rubber bands as I make my way back to the Knights of Arcadia hall. The last time I set foot in there, I was delivered bad news and then fell into bed with the person who made it happen. If what Devon says is true about Devil's Night, it's everything I want to change about the Knights. I'll be skating a fine line while serving on the committee.

We can leave the guy who's trying to get us all to Mars, but the outlandish show of money and sex needs to die a slow, painful death. We're better than that. We should lead with values over desires. If we do that, I think we can grow even further and beyond materialistic things.

It's making them see that—while also taking their toys away—that will be the most difficult part. In my eyes, they already started in the right direction when they agreed to give me a chance to make the Knights. Now that I'm here, I can continue to make changes. I might not be able to accomplish everything I want, but who knows? What about the girl after me? And the several girls after her?

The landscape will change. We just have to put in the work.

I enter the room Keegan told me to and come to a halt. Cameron is the only other person in the room. He peers up at me with one eye swollen shut, a hint of a purplish-blue bruise marring his usual good looks. "What happened to you?"

"*I* happened to him," a cold, familiar voice

announces from behind me. It's so recognizable because I've been spoken to with that same tone in the same dead octave. Turning, I find Keegan glaring at Cameron from the doorway. When he notices me looking at him, he comes up behind me to whisper firmly, "I've been blowing up your phone. Where the hell have you been?"

"Studying..." He's taken me so off guard that I actually answer the question. He never cares where I am.

He places his hand on my hip and squeezes. His touch is both comforting and insulting at the same time. It's like the wisp from a memory when all I wanted was for Keegan Forbes to touch me, but the dreaminess of the idea faded and grew into a harsh reality.

Leading me to a chair, he sits right next to me. I eye him warily, wondering what it is he's scheming at now by hovering. I can't believe he hit Cameron. He hasn't gotten into fights since he was a kid and his father knocked him out to teach him a "lesson." When Keegan finally came to, his father calmly explained that there would always be someone bigger around to take him down physically, so he should figure out other ways to get his point across.

It was a sick form of parenting then, and it's sick now.

"It was a sucker punch," Cameron fumes. "Next time, face me like a man."

"You're lucky that's all you got, asshole."

Cameron smirks. "Why? Because I was giving Delilah options?"

Keegan's hands turn to fists on the table. "She doesn't want anything you have to give her."

Ignoring their bravado nonsense, I pull out my phone. Oddly enough, it's turned off. When I power it back on, I have several missed texts and calls from him, so he wasn't lying about that. I peek out of the corner of my eye as more Knights enter the room. He's stock still, jaw flexing. Cameron must have really pissed him off in order for him to turn to his fists again.

I lean toward him. "I'm not your property you need to defend."

He shifts his gaze to mine. "Wrong, Dee. Completely and utterly wrong."

His words ring in my ear like a blaring siren while the room fills with more Knights. Some fledglings like Keegan and me and some a little older.

Darren Greene, a Knight who graduated last year, stands at the head of the table. "Good to see so many of you. Our Devil's Night reputation precedes us, I see. Gentlemen—" He quickly switches his gaze to me. "—and lady, welcome to the biggest night of the year... apart from graduation, of course."

The twinkle in his eyes, along with his words, makes me wonder just how depraved this night can get.

"Every year, fledglings and young Knights put together the biggest party of the year to impress the elders. If the party is fantastic, expect to receive accolades. If it lacks..." He grimaces charismatically. "Let's just say you won't be put on the Head Knight's Christmas card list. This isn't just another boring fundraising party. This is the party of the year where the Knights can be Knights. Where they can enjoy the spoils of their hard work. And yes, indeed, you will be judged. They expect a lot, so you better give them a lot."

When are we not being judged? The Knights are all about out-doing one another.

"In case you aren't yet aware, the main staples of the party are the lavish and interesting ways to get our guests to Dark Island, hot women, and luxurious decorations and festivities. I'm not going to tell you what's been done in previous years, so don't ask. At the end of the party, the elders will decide whether or not it exceeded their expectations. All the fledgling Knights will help, but it's up to this committee to plan the entire thing from start to finish. Don't miss out on any details. Trust me, the judges are particular."

He gives us all a winning smile before leaving the room. I blink after him. He was like one of those professors who "teaches" with monologue after monologue and then exits the room, believing he just did something deserving of a mic drop.

"How the hell are we supposed to do this?" Cameron whines. "I don't know a damn thing about throwing a party."

"What happened to your eye?" another Knight asks.

He scowls, and I speak up to transfer the attention away from him before he and Keegan get into it again. "Listen, he said we needed to plan the party and he wasn't going to tell us what has happened in previous years, but most of our fathers have been to this party, yes? We can ask them."

"Great idea," Keegan affirms. "We should all ask our fathers about previous years. I actually happened to sneak onto Dark Island during a couple of the parties, so I've seen a little."

"My dad's told me about them," Hunter Rothchild informs us with a sinister smirk. "Think a ton of sexy, naked women, rooms where we can go off to have sex with said naked women, and regular party shit."

If he says sex and naked women one more time...

"That lines up with my experience, too," Keegan relays. "There were a bunch of n—"

"Okay," I interrupt. "I think we've established the fact that there was a plethora of naked women."

"Jealous, Delilah?" Hunter asks. He has a disarmingly wide smile with an array of adorable freckles.

"Not in the slightest. I just don't think we're going to get extra credit for women in their birthday suits since it sounds like every Devil's Night has had that very same thing."

"But we can't skimp out on it either," Cameron argues. "If that's what they're used to, that's what they get."

"We should hold a contest." Keegan's eyes brighten. "We'll head to the local college, hold a wet t-shirt competition, or something similar, to recruit girls."

Hunter scratches his jaw. "We'll have to pay them handsomely. He never mentioned if we had a budget to work with or anything."

I run my hands through my hair, exasperated that all we're stuck on is the female entertainment. "He said we have to plan it from the ground up, so what would we do if this was our business?" I peer around the room, but they just stare at me, blinking, more than likely daydreaming about wet t-shirt contests. "We would decide what kind of budget we need and write up a proposal to the board. Jeez, do you guys have tits that much on the brain that you can't even think straight?"

Everyone laughs. Keegan even playfully nudges my knee with his before addressing the room again. "We can also get donations. He said this party was almost as big as graduation. We could get Armani to donate suits for door prizes, or Dior. What company like that wouldn't want to get their product in front of well...people like us?" He waits for them all to laugh, and then states, "Here's what we'll do." Keegan goes into CEO mode like he's been doing it his whole life. He tells them to question their families about previous Devil's Night parties, then instructs them to make a list of contacts they might have in prominent fashion and accessory companies. Finally, he finishes with informing them that they're to make a separate list of ideas for both getting the guests to the island and what we'll do when they get there.

"What about the actual event planning?" I ask. "Dishes, tablecloths, decorations..." I start listing all the different, finer details that make great foundations for parties, but that are also often overlooked.

"That sounds like a you job," he says.

"Sexist much?"

His lips thin. He locks gazes with me in a way that makes me think he's actually trying to figure me out. "We'll hire an event planner." Shrugging, he adds, "We'll need a theme first. Add that to your ideas list. We'll talk it out and vote next time we meet."

Honestly, if he weren't so dismissive, I would be attracted to the man who just took over the committee like he owned it. He took charge, and from eyeing everyone around the room, I can see they're deferring to him. I have no idea how the Forbes' men do it. It's like they get in a room and they can't help but take charge of it.

"Dee, take note of everyone in the room and start a text chain so we can contact each other if something comes up."

My stomach clenches. Everyone else is getting up from their chairs, ready to leave. There's no time to start something, but he's clearly addressed me like I'm the committee secretary.

Everyone leaves, and he notices I'm drilling holes into the side of his head. "What?" he snaps.

"I have to start the text chain? Should I have taken minutes too, Keegan? Come on."

"Give me a break. I asked because I figured you'd have everyone's number. You've had the same phone number for the longest time. Every guy I know has changed numbers at least a dozen times."

"I'm a part of this committee. You made sure of it, so the least you can do is realize I can do more than act like your personal secretary."

He runs his hand through his golden-brown hair. "You're a pain in my ass. First, I have to escort you to classes now because everyone knows you're a withering virgin, and now you're giving me shit for asking you to do something."

"There were six other people in the room. You could've asked any one of them to do it. But that's beside the point. Who said you could be boss?"

He grins. It's so malicious and cutting that there's no way it could be described as happy. "I'm always the boss, Delilah." He leans over to nip at my ear. "Remember that." He lets those words sink in before getting to his feet. "Now, come on. I've got to get you back to your room."

I open my mouth to argue, but in a way, this works in my favor. If Keegan and I could just stop picking fights, we might find a way to come to a truce. Each of us think we can't be what the other needs, but maybe that's because there's so much shit between us to wade through. The journey will be difficult, but if we get through it, the ending could be way better than we ever imagined.

"I accept your offer," I tell him.

"I wasn't offering. I was telling."

Or he could just be a control freak asshole.

11

What seems like a blink of an eye, Keegan goes from being an overbearing asshole to an overbearing—yet caring—asshole.

Last night alone, I received more texts from him than in the last year combined. Each of them was to check up on me.

Make sure your door is locked.

Call me if you need anything.

Are your windows locked?

The last one, though, shocked me. **Goodnight, Dee.**

I refused to answer the last because of the butterflies it gave me. He hadn't texted me 'goodnight' since the last time we officially dated. Instead of that bringing up bad memories like when he cheated, I remember all the good things about Keegan and I together. He was fun, caring. Sure, he could act aloof sometimes, but I figured that was because of his age, not because he lacked concern for me.

For the last couple of years, Keegan has been a stranger. The same boy I knew growing up, but it's almost as if he's worn different personalities. Since we broke up the last time, we haven't been on favorable talking terms, so I couldn't ask him what was wrong. If we're actually getting somewhere now, that might be a different story.

These thoughts roll through my head all throughout the next day. Half the time, I think about setting up a meeting with a therapist so I can exorcise the demon known as Keegan from my head. I'm aware I sound like the girl who wants to change a man, but I actually know Keegan better than that. It's like he's wearing clothes that aren't necessarily his. A cloak that makes him do things he wouldn't normally.

As for the committee task he gave me, I had to hunt down one guy's number, but I get the text thread going, sending them all a group message at the same time to announce that everyone who was at the meeting is included. However, I also take it a step further, reminding them of the plan we decided upon at the meeting. I specifically used *we*, trying to take the power out of Keegan's hands. Two *can* play this game. I'm not just going to sit to the side of the room and let the guys handle it. Sir Reginald wanted me to prove myself by being on this committee, so I'm going to do it to the best of my abilities.

My pep talk to myself doesn't last that long. Just enough time passes for Reginald's son to announce that he has an in with a few of the sorority leaders at the local college, and that they've agreed to start spreading the word that we're in need of "models" for a lavish, exclusive party.

My eyes nearly roll into the back of my head. Of course he has an in with sororities—plural. Do these guys even find time to study while fucking everything that walks?

Damn. I sound like Eden.

I take a deep breath after reading his message, but my phone buzzes in my hand as texts come through one after the other like a vibrating avalanche. It snowballs and snowballs, and before I can even put my two cents in, they've already arranged for a wet t-shirt contest to happen tonight at a dive bar in the local town. Yes, that's right. The future bigwigs of multimillion dollar companies will be judging a wet t-shirt contest. Somehow, I don't think that when our ancestors founded the Knights they envisioned their predecessors doing things like this. Did they hold wet hoopskirt contests? Maybe competitions on how tight women can pull their corsets? No, they were interested in values and work ethic and the joining of like minds.

I guess this means I have to be the best little wet t-shirt contest judge I can be. Even if it kills me inside.

I know as well as the rest of the guys that they're right about beautiful women attending Devil's Night. If that's what the elders have always had, they'll be expecting it, but maybe we can do something to make it more tasteful? A little less sex dungeon and more beautiful art?

I've been putting off calling my father to ask about past Devil's Nights, but I also don't want to be the only one going in blind. Instead of calling him on the phone and pretending as if we're having a normal father-daughter conversation, I decide to write him an email.

I pop into my favorite café. Tim's nowhere to be seen, even after I scour the place. Worry threads through me, and I can only hope he's still okay after getting jumped. A girl with a permanent scowl makes me my French vanilla cappuccino, and I take it back with me to the couch, so I can compose an email to my father that sounds as businesslike as possible while also asking about the less favorable side of the Knights.

Sipping my drink, I construct the email in my head first then punch it out on my phone's keyboard. By keeping my tone matter of fact, I won't be tempted to ask if he's ever taken one of the women into a sex room like the others suggested happened rampantly. Instead, I tell him I've made it onto the Devil's Night committee, and I need his help making sure I can make it the best party there is.

I hit Send and then down the rest of my cappuccino as if I can pretend that I didn't just ask my father about throwing a party full of debauchery since it's everything I want to fight against with the Knights.

"Need another?"

Startled, I spin, only to find Tim standing in front of me, a dish towel over his shoulder. I smile. "I didn't see you when I came in."

His brows rise. "You were looking for me?"

I take a closer look at him. The bruising has deepened today, making him look even worse. "I wanted to see if you were okay."

The coloring around his eyes can't hide the blush that tints his cheeks. "I'm fine. Really." Tilting his head toward me, his eyes drop to my phone in my hand and then back up. "What are you working on?"

I set my phone screen down on the table in front of me. "Nothing. Just emailing my dad."

He makes a face. "*Emailing* your dad? Most people I know don't email their dad."

I laugh at myself. Of course that would sound weird. "My dad's super busy. Sometimes the only way I can get ahold of him is to email his work." At least, that's what I'm telling this guy. I'm sure he'd look at me like I have two heads if he knew I was going to judge a wet t-shirt contest tonight.

I groan inwardly again. Just why?

My phone buzzes, and I flip my phone around to peek at the screen. **Are you safe?**

"Sorry, I have to respond to this." Picking my phone up, I type out: **Yes. All good. About to head to the library.**

Studying is the last thing I want to do right now, but since my life is being consumed by planning a party I don't want to attend but could reinforce my membership into the Knights, I have to study when I can. Standing, I straighten my shoulders and place my phone into my bag. I nearly jump when Tim's rumbling voice says, "On the house."

Peering up, I find my new friend holding out a to-go cup. "For me?"

"You look like you need it."

He has no idea. I take it from him with a smile. "Thank you."

"No problem." He shrugs. "And you know, if you ever want to chat or get together when I'm not working, let me know."

"I'll do that," I tell him, wondering why there aren't more guys like him around before dipping out to study my butt off.

I finish all my coursework in record time, speed reading through textbooks and praying I've retained everything. When I'm done, I dress for tonight's festivities. Keegan sends me a text, asking me if I actually plan on going to the judging tonight. My response is curt and tells him just how excited I am. **Of course. I figure I can afford to lose a few brain cells tonight.**

He responds back with: **Ha. Ha.**

Unbeknownst to me, Keegan shows up just as I'm leaving. He's dressed down in a pair of jeans and a feather red shirt that hugs his pectorals. He blinks in surprise when we run into each other in the foyer of my dorm. "You look...good, Dee."

I'm wearing a distressed jean skirt with a pair of leggings underneath. My custard yellow shirt shows off a hint of stomach as I make my way toward him. "What are you doing here?"

"I figured we could ride together."

I chuckle at him. "No need to worry. No one's asked me if I needed help with my virginity problem all day today."

He relaxes a little, and it surprises me that he cares so much. It's not in the way I want him to. Not yet, anyway. I'm pretty sure he's only worried about protecting his prized possession at the moment.

I took care to dress the way I did tonight. Devon's

words were in my head the entire time, telling me that in Keegan's eyes, I might not be making an effort in ways that he can see. So, I chose an outfit I believed would fit in most in a dive bar in the downtown area. In addition to that, I'm wearing big, hoop earrings with my hair in long, beachy waves.

"Better safe than sorry."

I bite my tongue, refusing to start a fight by asking him where that attitude was the other day when he decided he was going to tell Anne-Marie that I'm still sporting the v-card. I've decided that even though I don't like Anne-Marie, she was right. I don't think Keegan intended to tell anyone. He let his temper get the best of him, and it slipped. It doesn't excuse him by any means, but I can understand it.

The ride into town is quiet and comforting. The engine on his muscle car thrums underneath us as he steers the car down twisting roads. When winter comes, he'll have to put this vehicle in storage, so he can start driving his Jeep.

The dark night creeps in. Wind blows the colored leaves on the trees haphazardly. Keegan reaches down to turn the heat up when he notices me rubbing my arms. "You know you don't have to do this. You're going to hate it."

"You wanted me on the committee, I'm on the committee. I'm joining in, being a part of the group.

How would it look if I only did part of the planning?"

His jaw ticks. The blue light from the car's dashboard illuminates his high cheekbones along with his clear frustration. "You're beginning to make me regret talking to Reginald Wright after all."

Wow. That's rich. "Why? Because it was wrong? Or because you don't want me around when you're out having fun with the guys?"

He shakes his head, fingers clenching the wheel. "Why are you always so bitchy?"

"I could ask the same thing about you, you know. You expect me to just take things sitting down, and I won't."

He moves his head from side to side as if he's trying to stretch his neck. I know what this is about. He wants me to cater to his every word like most girls do. Other girls don't dream of talking back to him, even if he is acting like a jerk. It's not being bitchy though. It's having self-respect.

Minutes pass where he doesn't respond, so I decide to change the subject. "I was thinking about a theme. I haven't heard back from my dad yet, so I'm not sure if this has been done in the past, but what about devils versus angels? All the girls can wear white, maybe even with feather wings? It's the day before Halloween, so costumes would coincide with that."

"Angel outfits? Like Victoria's Secret?"

I shrug. "Yeah, I guess."

He sucks his lip into his mouth in concentration. A moment later, he says, "I like it. Actually, I think it's perfect." Before I can get too big of a head, he tacks on, "The guys will love it. Everyone gets turned on by the idea of sullying something perfect."

He cuts his gaze to the vee of my legs, and I crush my thighs together at the influx of heat. The temperature in my entire body rises until the heat from the air vents blowing on me is too much. I don't understand how he can do this to me with just one look.

His stare lingers for way too long, but then he asks, "Should the guys wear red or black?"

Excellent. Something I can concentrate on other than wanting Keegan so bad it hurts. "I was wondering about that too. Black is more traditional. It's the opposite of white as opposed to red, which we would only be using because of fairytale-like portrayals of the devil."

"I say black then."

"We have to pitch it to the group, Keegan," I remind him.

He shakes his head. "That's where you're wrong, Delilah. You don't understand the power couple we could be. We could make anything happen. Half the time, I think that's why you don't want anything to do with me. You fear us together."

"That's...not true. Keegan, I—" I stop myself from telling him what I have a few times before. It's never stopped being true, but sometimes love isn't enough. Sometimes it warps into something awful. "There's still hope for us, I think. I'm not scared of it."

He turns into town and parks the car in a public lot. I've been through the tourist laden town enough to know that the dive bar is only a couple of blocks from here, however the main street is usually full of cars, so it's better to walk in.

"I hope you're right," he says, his voice so low I wonder if I actually heard him at all. He exits the car, and I step out after him. We walk side-by-side down the sidewalk. At the entrance to the bar ahead of us, a few girls enter in white half shirts. Keegan smiles. "This is going to be fun."

I roll my eyes. "It's disgusting."

"You don't have to be here," he presses.

"*You* made sure I had to, but that's fine," I tack on. "Maybe I'll find some guys in there to hire, too."

Keegan pulls to a stop. "What?"

Snickering, I turn toward him. "Fair's fair, right? There's a girl in the Knights now, and not to mention that there are a few Knights who swing the other way.

We should have a few guys, too. Are there wet bikini contests for guys?"

He growls low in his throat, but any argument he's decided to make is cut off when Cameron comes up behind us. He slaps Keegan on the shoulder and winks at me. "Looking hot, Delilah. Wish you were participating."

I'd rather cut my own eyeballs out. Instead of saying that, I glare at him. Laughing boisterously, he walks inside. Keegan grabs my hand territorially, and we follow him into the bar.

Music is in full swing. Neon lights strobe over the main areas of the room while the corners stay in shadow. A musty smell I'm not particularly keen on tickles my nostrils, but the good news is, it looks like they've shut down the entire bar for the competition. No doubt the owners are well aware that the rich kids from Carnegie will buy copious amounts of alcohol, so it's worth more to shut it down than open up for everyone.

Judging by the way tables are already filled with full and half empty drinks, they made the right decision. Cameron, and a couple of the other guys, are lining up a row of chairs to face the stage. Behind the raised platform is a wall of mirrors, so we'll literally be able to see everything.

Nerves flutter in my stomach. I don't really care

about seeing the girls in their t-shirts. I'm for body positivity and all that, but I worry about what they're getting themselves into.

I pull back on Keegan's sleeve before he can make a getaway to the real fun already happening. "Hey, I was thinking. When we hire these girls, we should make sure they know what they're getting into ahead of time."

Keegan drifts his hand up to play with the ends of my hair. "Don't worry. They know. Plus, we'll add it to the contract along with the confidentiality agreement. If they don't want to get buried, they'll do as the contract says."

I swallow, still not liking the idea. Who's looking out for the girls if it's a one-sided contract?

"Dee, this has happened for so many years. There's never been a problem. It doesn't need to be fixed, and you certainly don't need to worry about it."

Fine. The least I can do is help these girls not parade around in nothing though. If the rest of the committee likes my devils versus angels idea, I can at least put them in white lingerie.

"Now, relax," Keegan tells me. "You might learn a thing or two."

My jaw snaps shut, and I want to wipe the smirk that follows off his face.

12

I've never seen so many breasts in my life.

I've also never been witness to so many horny twenty something year olds making spectacles of themselves while drooling over said breasts.

Music pumps through the speakers, and lights flash like we're at a disco. The dive bar is filled with electricity, appearing livelier than when we first walked in. Like Keegan told me, the girls are absolutely fine with strutting their stuff on stage. Some of them have real dancing talent while others just prance around, trying to look as sexy as possible. Painted numbers adorn their shoulders so we can judge without bias. However, it also kind of feels like we don't care enough to learn their names.

Regardless, I have a sneaking suspicion that my

picks will be far different from the other guys on the committee.

Unfazed that I'm sitting right next to him, Keegan enjoys the overtly sexual display with the others, whooping and hollering for his favorites. As the night wears on, the final girls turn bolder, probably desperate to be chosen. After all, they will be paid handsomely for this. One girl, whose hair is dyed in mermaid colors, saunters up to us, giving each guy a private dance. She doesn't get to me because Keegan pulls her onto his lap, keeping her firmly in place while yelling out for the sorority leaders to let the next girl on stage.

I guess she's going to stay there then?

I glare over at the two of them. She appears content as can be sitting on my future husband's lap. He runs his hands up and down her spine before peering over at me. When he sees me looking, he traces designs over her skin until she arches her back.

I can't help but think this is in retaliation for not giving in to him yet. He's trying to make me jealous, so I'll get on my knees and beg, just like he wants.

I count down the seconds as she stays there. Three girls come up and finish, and I haven't even scored them on my sheet because my body is consumed with angry heat. I *am* jealous. I want to rip her off his lap and stake my claim. I want his fingers so deep inside me again that I scream his name.

When he starts to massage her knee, I'm out. I stand, marching toward the bathrooms, avoiding the bar waitresses who are keeping us steadily supplied with alcohol. I haven't drank one yet. Not because I don't enjoy a drink now and then, but because I'm doing a job.

Just my luck, the wet t-shirt girls have inhabited the bathroom. They're all laughing and cleaning up, talking about how much fun dancing for us was. How freeing. A few of them even discuss how hot the panel of judges was, and clearly, they're not talking about me.

"I hope I get picked," I hear.

"Girl, me too. I need help paying the rest of the year's tuition." She lowers her voice. "My sister got picked one year. She got paid a shitton of money." I take note of the number on her shoulder. I can't recall whether or not I gave her a good score, but I'll damn well make sure I do when I get back to my chair.

Since the bathroom is a bust, and I don't really need to go anyway, I head back out. I watch the remaining girls from behind the curtains as they wait to own the stage. Right before they enter, a girl, who I'll guess is the president of one of the sororities, pours a pitcher of water over their chests. Some want just their shirts soaked through, others ask for it all the way from the top of their head.

Peeking around the curtain, I stare up at the line of

Knights. Mermaid girl is still perched on Keegan's lap. She's turned around now, blocking his view of the contestant who's performing for him right now. My blood boils. He's not even doing his job. He can't even be serious about this. To top it all off, he's doing it to hurt me.

Well, he said I could learn a thing or two, didn't he? I think I have.

I waltz back into the bathroom, exclaiming, "I need a white shirt." The girls stop and peer at me. Giving them a tiny smile, I say, "Sorry, I forgot mine."

If they recognize me from being on the judging panel, they don't say anything.

One woman rifles through her bag. "All I have is this one." It's a full-length, white t-shirt, the kind found in packs of three or ten at huge department stores. "But..." she tacks on. "...I also have these."

She pulls out a pair of scissors.

"You're the best," I gush.

Taking them both from her, I cut off the sleeves, making the arm holes a fashion statement rather than boring, tidy lines. Then, I cut the very bottom of the shirt off before pushing through the crowd and side-stepping makeup piles littered like land mines on the floor to find an empty stall. I throw my shirt and bra over the divider and pull on the white one, tying it just under my breasts into a cute little side knot.

My fingers shake as nerves run through me like galloping gazelles. I bite my lip as I toe off my shoes and socks, leaving them there on the floor. Everything in me is telling me to do this, to give Keegan a taste of his own medicine, yet...maybe it's not about that at all. Maybe it's about letting my hair down for once. I'm a trained dancer. I can out-dance most of the girls that I've seen so far, and if I happen to make Keegan jealous as fuck in the process, then so be it.

The only problem I can see is that I don't want any of the other Knights to know it's me. They'll be sworn to secrecy because what happens on Knight business stays Knight business. However, I don't want this to be a memory in some of these asshole's heads when I enter my career. Years from now, we could all be at the same fancy party and I don't want these douches remembering what my breasts look like in a wet t-shirt.

I whip the door open and step out, my mind still nudging me with reasons to move forward. I just watched all of these girls step up to the plate. It would be counterproductive *not* to follow after them. To think myself above them. I'm a supporter of women doing whatever they want. It's not really them that I judge, it's the guys who think up this bullshit.

Grimacing, I take in the room before asking, "Anyone have a mask? I don't really want to show my face."

"I do," a feminine voice calls out. Her shirt is still stuck to her breasts, but her ensemble was the most proper we'd seen out of the girls. She grins. "I was in Phantom of the Opera as one of the masquerade guests. I just happen to have the mask I wore." Digging through a brown bag at her feet, she picks through its contents until she holds out a red lace mask that covers both eyes and a section of one cheek.

"Thank you." I pull it on and check the bathroom mirror. The cheek section of the mask simulates flames as I move my head back and forth. It looks like my face is on fire.

"They probably won't pick you if you put on a mask though," the girl offers tentatively like she might be crushing my hopes and dreams.

"That's okay," I tell her. "I'm doing this for me."

"It's so liberating," a girl from the back speaks up. "I was really nervous, too, but it wasn't as bad as I thought. They were really into it."

I nod, knowing she's right. I had a front row seat for all of it.

With my black leggings and tied off shirt, I look like a dancer. My taut, lean stomach that never went away from years of ballet practice is on display. From the outside, I appear calm and pulled together, but nerves are gathering, tightening the muscles in my core.

To hide my hair, I throw it up in a bun. With the

lights and the shadows, I highly doubt anyone will know it's actually me. If Keegan realizes, that will be the satisfying part.

"You better hurry up, girl. They're winding down."

I run out of the bathroom and get in line. There are only two girls in front of me, and they don't dance for long. Two minutes, tops.

When I get to the front of the line, the sorority president lifts her brows at my mask. I shrug, and she responds in kind. I guess neither one of us care that much. "Where do you want it?" she asks as another sorority girl hands her the pitcher of water. I'd rather have her dump it over my head, so my breasts aren't entirely exposed, but if I go back out there afterward with wet hair, the Knights will know.

"My chest," I tell her, butterflies fluttering in my stomach like antsy bees.

"Here," she says. She sets down the pitcher and picks up a pair of scissors next to her feet. "You'll thank me." She pulls my collar forward and starts cutting a V-neck into my shirt. The point of the vee settles between my bare breasts. Completely embarrassed now, I almost walk away. Before I can bow out, though, she throws the water at my chest and pushes me toward the stage.

I'm under the lights before I know it. The song pulses through speakers over my head. I stand there like a deer in the headlights for a split second before my body takes over through dance. I don't look down at my shirt, but I feel myself nipping, the soaked fabric clinging to my breasts. They're getting quite the show, that's for sure.

For a moment, the crowd is eerily quiet before the guys start cheering. I pirouette across the stage, leap into the air and land on what happens to be the beat of the song. It's almost as if I planned it that way. I stand, using the side of the stage as my focal point instead of the judges as I move to the music across the wooden floor. I throw myself into leaps and turns. The music overhead turns sultry, and I flow with it, dancing my fingers across the side of my breasts down my front and to my hips where I roll my body to the beat.

The Knights go crazy. No one shouts my name. I haven't blown my cover, which makes me move even freer. I chance a look toward them, and gratefully, find the lights in my face blind me.

On a sexy, supercharged high, I leap into the air, landing softly while I lower to my knees, forcing myself into a full split before pulling my legs back behind me and arching my back, ending in a position that drives them all crazy.

The lights dim, and for a split second, I tell myself not to look, not to chance the gazes on their faces. But the other girls were right. This *is* powerful. I make myself peer at them. It's easier since they don't know who I am. I watch their faces, their hooded eyes. One by one, I survey them, my pulse jumping at my wrists. When I get to the end, Keegan is scowling at me. The girl he had on his lap is nowhere to be seen. Strength charges through my veins, and I give him a wink before getting up and sashaying across the stage, leaving it all behind me.

A few of the girls bring me in for a hug when I get off stage. I hold them tightly, feeling the solidarity amongst us. It was only a couple of minutes, but it was amazing. They were right. It was like taking the power that I thought they had over me by acting like a bunch of oversexed barbarians and turning it in my favor. They were eating out of the palm of my hand. They *wanted* me.

I just release the last girl when a strong hand grips my wrist from behind. I'm tugged away, down a hallway that's the same kind of rough around the edges as the rest of the bar. Keegan doesn't say a word as he yanks me into a room in the back, slamming the door behind us.

"Whoa," a male voice protests. "You can't be back here."

Keegan takes out his wallet. He grabs a fistful of hundreds and throws them on the desk the plump man sits at. "Actually, I can. Give us a minute."

The man doesn't balk. He takes the wad of cash, sticks it in his pocket, and tips his invisible hat to Keegan.

"What the hell?" I ask, pulling my wrist away when the door closes behind the retreating man. Keegan twists the lock, clicking the metal into place with a hard thwack.

"*What the hell?*" he repeats. He bites his lips while looking down my shirt. It's the first time I peer down. My breast shape clearly comes into view. The wet shirt leaves nothing to the imagination. I can even see the darkened areola. "You just bared yourself to the rest of the Knights. You're lucky they didn't realize it was you." He snaps the mask off my face, and the elastic breaks. Reaching out, he undoes my hair, and the wavy, blonde strands fall to my shoulders. When his gaze falls to my chest, he breathes out. "Jesus, Delilah."

"If everyone else didn't know it was me, how did you?"

"You think I wouldn't? You think I haven't memorized every curve of your body? Or the way that you move? It was blindingly obvious from the moment you stepped on stage," he grinds out. "Showing everyone what's mine..."

"And yet, you give away freely what's mine," I counter, breathing heavily. "You did it on purpose, and this is the consequence."

Still high on power because of the way his eyes scorch right through me, I trail my fingers down his chest until they sit at the top of his jeans. Beneath my touch, his muscles contract.

"You want me and only me," I tell him. "That's why you let that girl go. Admit it to yourself." My fingers brush across his taut skin. "Stop trying to make me jealous."

"It's the only way I get your attention."

"You want my attention?" I flick the button on his jeans loose and lower the zipper. Reaching inside, I grab his straining cock, fisting it with my fingers. Tentatively, I run my hand toward his base and back. He bucks forward. "She doesn't mean anything to you, but I do," I accuse. "That's why you ran to confront me. To tell me I was bad."

"To claim what's mine," he argues.

"Then I'll claim what's mine." I lower to my knees, bringing his jeans and boxers with me. His erect dick juts toward my mouth. The head of his cock oozes pre-cum, and I lick my lips in preparation. Control gallops through my veins, especially when his abdominal muscles constrict, and his hips make a circular motion like he can barely restrain himself. I have him right where I want him. He's usually thinking me, me, me, and he still is, but right now, it's at my command. My doing.

I should've known he wouldn't let it stay that way though. He grabs my head, tightening his grip on my hair at the back of my skull. "Open your mouth and take it like a bad girl," he demands.

I peek up at him, riveted by the desire in his eyes. Slowly, I open my mouth, parting my lips ever so carefully, letting him know that I'll do it, but it'll still be on my terms. As soon as there's enough room, he shoves his cock forward. He pitches ahead so hard I nearly gag, but I dismiss the urge, taking him in under his illusion of control.

The more I pleasure him, the more he loses it. He drops his head against the door as I stretch my lips around his base, sucking. "Fuuuuck."

I moan in encouragement, grabbing his hips to steady myself. It takes a few passes to get used to his size, but I listen, I learn, I follow his movements until I take them up a notch.

"Christ, Dee. Suck my dick. Fuck yes. Take all of it."

I do, again and again. My lips pass over his hard ridges while my tongue sweeps over his fleshy head, catching all the salty pre-cum from his tip.

"I miss watching you dance, Dee. Watching you jump through the air, so free, so fucking beautiful it hurts."

I stutter, and his grip on my crown increases, making me keep the pace while he reveals his soul.

"I would know your body anywhere. Recognize that look of peace on your face as you twirl, so light on your feet like a goddamn goddess." He rolls his hips forward, and I relax my throat to take him all in.

He fucks my mouth, moaning. I cling to his words, to the outright revelation of his feelings. My eyes start to tear. I had no idea he thought of me like that, that he remembered the little things. With so much shit between us, it was easier to think he'd completely changed. That, somehow, I was still trying to put a stranger into the box of my first love. I was wrong. My body overheats, the only thing swimming through my brain is to make him cum.

"Your fucking mouth, babe." He catches my gaze, and I sigh over him.

He picks up the pace, forcing his cock between my lips. I press my mouth firmly over him, watching as he loses control.

"Fuck me, Delilah Astor. Those pretty lips. That perfect face." With a restrained cry, he forces his hips forward one last time, ending in a long, hard groan. Rivulets of cum stream from his slit, hitting the back of my throat. I do everything I can to swallow and keep swallowing until he shudders to a stop.

He collapses against the door, and I follow after,

giving him one more deep throat before backing off, his semi-hard dick bobbing from my mouth. Pleasure coats me in a warm blanket. Pride seeps through my pores. I brought Keegan Forbes to his knees, figuratively. He just gave me more truths in the last few minutes than he has in years.

There is still hope for the two of us.

13

*T*he girls clear out of the bar after the last girl performs. I hurry, changing back into my regular clothes, attempting to not look like I was just up on stage with my boobs hanging out. Thankfully, the wide, wall-length mirror in the now empty bathroom allows me to make sure I'm carefully put back together before I head back out to the main bar.

Taking in a deep breath, I force myself to relax. A nervous person always draws more attention than a confident one. However, when I get out there, I find there was no need to worry in the first place. The rest of the guys on the committee aren't even paying attention to what I'm doing. The waitresses fill up their drinks while they joke with one another.

The only person who even notices me walking toward them is Keegan. His eagle-eyed stare zeroes in on me. For once, in what seems like a long time, he's paying more attention to me than what's going on around him. With his hands in his pockets, he stands there casually. His whole look tonight screams modern James Dean, and I am here for it.

I'm so caught up in the ferocity of Keegan's gaze that I almost miss Cameron's snide comment. "Where've you been, Astor? Chicken out?"

I give him a smirk. "I see my own breasts every day, I'm pretty sick of them to be honest."

A few of the guys snicker, but it's time to get down to judging. With the party only a couple of weeks away, there's too much to do to bicker. I take my place on an empty chair next to Keegan. They've rearranged all the seats around a table, so we all sit peering at one another. Before Keegan can even attempt to take over the meeting, I speak up. "There's no reason to sit around talking about it. We only need one person to count the votes and contact the girls who made it through. We saw seventy-five girls. That's way too many to hire when our guest list isn't even that much. What's a good number?"

"Fifty," Keegan states.

"Great. Who volunteers to count the votes and reach out?"

They all glance at each other. I sit back and wait for them to figure it out amongst themselves because I refuse to volunteer. I started the text chain, made it to this display of male testosterone, and begrudgingly emailed my father. No one can say I haven't done my part so far.

In addition to all that, I learned one important lesson. Something Keegan probably didn't dream of inadvertently passing on. Withholding sex can be powerful, but so can being sexual.

"I'll do it," Cameron huffs.

"Great," I announce, not giving him a chance to back out of it. "We'll meet Monday to discuss what we found out from our fathers, and we'll go from there."

Glassy stares eye me before nodding. Their hesitation isn't alcohol induced. It's been this way my entire life. Dudes aren't used to hearing women boss them around. Luckily, that never stopped me from doing so.

"Sweet." Sir Reginald's son stands. Shoving his beer bottle in the air with a war cry, he shouts, "Party time!"

As if on cue, the music turns up again. I have zero desire to party with these guys in this fashion, so I lean over to Keegan. "I'll get an Uber."

His possessive eyes lock me in place. "The fuck you will."

I study him. Surprisingly, I find no residual effects of alcohol consumption. His eyes aren't hazed over like the other committee members. There's no slurring or an increased time to string his thoughts together. While the other Knights are too busy to notice, I place my hand on Keegan's thigh and lean toward him. I don't want to fight but remaining at this bar while a bunch of guys drink themselves into comas isn't my idea of a good time. "I'm not staying here, Keegan."

He squeezes my hand and stands from his seat. Grabbing his keys from his pocket, he says, "I'm not asking you to."

I lift my brows in surprise. It's been a while since he's done something chivalrous for me. Following him to my feet, we say goodbye to the others before exiting the bar. The streets are speckled with people finding places to drink tonight. Loud music echoes out of several different venues as we make our way toward Keegan's vehicle.

When we finally get in the car, he takes a deep breath, leaning his head back on the headrest. "You're lucky they didn't know it was you."

I shrug. I was pretty sure they wouldn't find out, but I'm also relieved. Facing them after that wouldn't have been fun. "I know."

"You could've just told that girl to get off my lap, you know." He starts the car, and it roars to life, startling me.

"And embarrass you in front of the Knights?"

"Embarrass me?" He shakes his head. "No,

Delilah, it's not embarrassing. They know we're ending up together. The only people who don't know are outsiders."

"You didn't have to pull her onto your lap either," I counter.

"Sure, I did. That's just the kind of person I am."

My lips are still worn from having his dick shoved down my throat, so I don't appreciate his answer. "Listen here, Keegan Forbes. If you want to go anywhere near me again, you'll knock your shit off. I *don't* share. I'm not going to be your perfect little housewife who sits around muted when you say dumb shit or come home smelling like another woman."

"Yet, you do now."

He presses down on the accelerator, and we fly through town, rolling through stop signs and roaring through the back roads as we turn toward Carnegie. The whole drive, I sit there with my nails digging into my thighs. He drives with a fierceness, a domineering control over the machine, and I wonder if the way he's driving is him trying to gain back a little authority from what he feels like he lost in the office.

Also, he knows I hate it when he drives this fast.

The vehicle comes to a squealing stop in the lot closest to my dorm. I whip my seatbelt off and face him. "You're trying to push my buttons. Well, get over it, Keegan. You know how I feel about you. Do you think I've done anything like that before? Do you—?"

"Actually, I've been meaning to ask. How *did* you learn how to suck dick that good?"

I gnash my teeth together, my heart beating like a rabid animal in my chest. His first reaction is to argue—to fight. I once heard my dad say that the Forbes never start an argument they can't win. Maybe I'm onto something here. When Keegan feels as if he's lost his edge, he does a one-eighty, turning into the guy who can decimate others with a few words. "I took my cues from you," I tell him softly. "When you moaned, when you gripped my hair so hard it felt like you were going to rip it from my scalp, I knew I was doing a good job. You. Broke. And that's—"

He clenches his fingers around the steering wheel, knuckles turning white. "Get out."

I blink, not expecting the pure venom in his voice. Sure, we're fighting, but I thought we might finally be getting somewhere.

"Get the fuck out!" he screams, punching the steering wheel.

I feel for the door handle, and when I find the cool piece of metal, I yank it open and practically spill out of the car. I'm barely clear when he guns the engine, taking off in the middle of the parking lot. The passenger side door isn't even shut, but he takes a curve ahead so fast that it bangs against the hinges and finally closes.

Trembling, I get to my feet. With Keegan, it's one step forward, two steps back. He has some sort of mental block on getting close to me. I'm sick of stepping on eggshells around each other. Pulling my phone out, I attempt to call him. It goes straight to voicemail. I'm sure his fancy car has Bluetooth, so he's avoiding me. The echo of his revving engine reverberates around campus as I walk toward my dorm, dejected.

When he calms down, he and I have to get to the bottom of this. Either he wants to be with me or he doesn't. I'm sick of waiting around, carefully peeling his layers back one at a time.

I send him a text just inside the vestibule of my dorm. **When you find the boy who saved me from drowning, send him my way.**

Those innocent, blue eyes. They're still in there somewhere.

My calf muscles ache as I walk up the steps. It's been too long since I've done any of those ballet moves. I'm sure they were far from perfect, which makes the words Keegan spoke to me even more special. He recognized me through my dance, and he's right about one thing. When I dance, the most honest, raw parts of me rise to the surface. It's like bleeding in front of everyone, and the fact that he picked up on that, regardless of the stunt he just pulled, it has to mean something.

A year from now, I'll probably be cursing myself for still having faith in Keegan Forbes, but when you've been in love with a guy for as long as I have, it's not easy to give up.

When I get to the top of the stairs, I slow. A bouquet of flowers lies in front of my door. My name is scrawled across a note that's attached to the front. I don't recognize the handwriting. It's choppy and staccato as if someone wrote it in a rush.

I pick up the flowers, peering inside at the odd, inner pattern of the paper that holds the flowers together. It's too shadowy in the hall to see clearly, so I walk inside my room and flick on the light. Placing my purse on the bed, I head toward the dresser to unwrap the array of multi-colored roses. It takes me a moment for my eyes to ascertain what I'm looking at. Once I do, I gasp. The usual, thin sheet of plastic that wraps bouquets is still there, but the pattern comes from a picture of me, spread out on a yacht in my bikini.

Every inch of me is practically blown up. The freckle on my inner shoulder. The dip of my lips. Even a bead of sweat clinging to my chest. My nipples are as hard as pebbles. It's hard to tell if it's doctored or if I was actually nipping that much.

Pixelated and zoomed, I'm aghast at what I see in

front of me. My every damn curve on display. I rip the picture out and turn it over to find the opposite side has an article about famous celebrity couples. The damn thing is from a paparazzi mag where corporations with too much money pay for pictures they shouldn't have. Obviously, this picture was taken while I was on my father's yacht over break.

Stepping back, I try to wrap my head around it all. Why I got these flowers, and why the hell the person stuck a picture of me from a magazine in the bouquet. Like this is some funny joke or something. I let the paper go, needing to put distance between me and it when something falls to the floor with a plop.

I jump back, only to realize it's not an insect that's going to scurry toward me. It's something much different. When the thing finally comes into focus, I throw my hands over my mouth in shock. Dread deadens my limbs.

Holy fuck. Holy fuck, no.

It's a condom. A *used* condom.

A squeak pours from my mouth. The scene before me is vomit-inducing. My stomach roils, but I pull it together with anger. Snatching the envelope off the paper, I rip it open with shaking fingers, wondering who's going to fess up to this. One of these narcissistic assholes I go to school with thinks it's funny to drop used condoms in bouquets.

However, the interior of the card takes the cake.

I was thinking about you. Getting ready for your big day. Trust me, I've memorized every part of your body, Delilah Astor. I'm ready.

Getting ready for me? The condom?

Trembling fingers reach to cover my mouth. It's as if the world turns upside down. I stagger back, hitting the bed. When I feel my purse, I search for my phone, staring at the disgusting gift in panic.

The only person I can think to call just left me, but I don't care.

It rings to voicemail. I call again. It goes to voicemail once more. I leave one, telling him to fucking call me now.

The third time I call, he picks up. "Christ, Dee. I don't want to talk to—"

A mixture of angry, fearful tears spring to my eyes. "Come back," I croak out, emotion clogging my throat. As soon as I hear his voice, the stress of what's happening crashes down on me, and I can't stop it. It's like the dam breaks.

"Delilah," he growls, clearly not in the mood for any of this.

"Come back," I whimper. "Someone left me something disgusting." I take a deep breath. These next words have never been more true. "I need you."

"What?" The car comes to a screeching halt in the background. "What is it? Fuck. I'll be right there."

"It's... it's..." I'm staring right at everything, but I can't put it into words. The line goes dead in my hand. Lowering the phone, I keep a death grip on it like it's a lifeline.

My gaze darts around the room while I wait for him to show. Clearly, whoever left this didn't make it inside. I can feel good about that, except I brought it into my space. No matter how hard I try not to, I keep staring at the condom, the words written on the card spiraling through my head.

This is obviously because of my virginity. Keegan will tell me it's just some joke one of these playboy assholes are playing with me, and that will be it. He'll tell me it's nothing to worry about and that I'm over-reacting.

Except, that's not the case at all. Keegan's thunderous footsteps storm up the steps a few minutes later. My door flies open, and he darts his gaze around the room before finding the obvious culprits. He picks up the note, his gaze furiously eating up the words. He drops it almost immediately, his hands turning to fists. "Fucking assholes. I'll kill them."

"Who?"

"I don't care who. I'll burn them all to the ground." He studies the flowers, the picture, and it's then that he notices the condom. Whipping his gaze toward me, his white-hot fury is on display. "This was in there?"

I nod numbly. "In the paper. When I was trying to see what was on the picture, it fell out."

Tears track down my cheeks. Keegan marches over, pulling me to my feet in an embrace that I go into willingly. He wraps his arms around me tightly, and I shiver at the thought of someone jerking off to my picture in that stupid magazine. No one cares about me. At least, no one should. People only know who I am because I'm rich. How pathetic is that? It's not as if I've cured diseases or won a gold medal in the Olympics, or hell, done anything exciting with my life —yet. I'm nobody.

"It's okay," Keegan reassures. He rubs a reassuring hand up and down my spine. "I'll take care of it. I'm so sorry, Delilah. So fucking sorry." His fingers curl into my skin, almost as if he could crawl inside me if he could. The twinge of pain is reassuring, helping me stay tethered to the moment.

"What are we going to do?" I ask. As with anything that happens to people like us, it's a game to figure out what to share with people. I don't want to be the girl who got a threatening note and have it splashed all over the news. There are the Knights to think about, too. My family. My school. They won't want any of that publicity.

What I hate most is that I have to think about any of this. Why does my mind immediately go into clean up mode?

"This is bad," I say, voice breaking again.

"I'll take care of it. I'll call my—"

"No," I blurt. "We're not calling your dad. It's too fucking embarrassing. We'll call mine."

"*I'll* call yours," he affirms. "You're doing nothing, but staying right next to me, so I can kill anyone who comes close to you."

I grip him, and for a flash of a second while we stare into one another's eyes, I see the innocent boy I knew when we were kids. It's only there for a brief, wonderful moment, but here Keegan is again, saving my life.

"First, I'm taking you to my room," he informs me. "You don't need to see this right now. I'll call your dad from my place."

Keegan rubs my arms as he steps away. After grabbing my purse, he follows me down the stairs. It's super late. No one else is around, so it feels like we're two convicts trying to escape.

"I'm going to take care of you," Keegan whispers against my temple while we walk toward the parking lot.

I take a deep breath as he helps me into the car. The short drive to his residence hall goes by quickly with his hand in mine. Just as he promised, he takes me up to his room. The penthouse, of course. Three walls in his bedroom have antique, arch shaped windows. The room itself is much larger than mine, furnished with refined taste.

Once he settles me on the bed, he goes into the bathroom. The faucet turns on, and his muffled voice makes it back into this room, but I can't hear what's being said until he walks back out. "She's fine. She's with me." He nods as he listens to whoever is on the other side of the line before finishing with, "Let me know."

I blink at him after he hangs up. "Was that my dad?"

His gaze collides with mine. A mixture of worry and stark confidence shines through. "He's taking care of it."

I close my eyes, relief flooding me. My dad will take care of everything. He always does.

Keegan reaches out his hand. My stomach flip flops at his show of vulnerability. "I drew you a bath. I even dropped in one of those bath bombs that my mother packs for me every semester."

A slow smile curves my lips. He glances to the side, shaking his head. It's as if he can barely stand to look at me. My stomach squeezes. "Keegan?"

"I'm fucked up, Dee. Sometimes I don't even know what the fuck is wrong with me."

"Shh," I tell him. I feel like I have the right boy back at the exact right moment that I need him.

He grabs my cheeks, making me look at him. "Don't you dare comfort me right now. Don't you fucking dare."

He breathes out heavily before walking away. With his back to me, I spy the heaviness in his shoulders. When he doesn't turn for the longest time, I slip past him, entering the steamy bathroom with my heart in my throat.

14

I wake in Keegan's bed of all places. My hair still smells like vanilla lavender from the bath bomb. Next to me, the bed is cold, so I roll over to look for him. Crumpled sheets lie next to the bed along with a single pillow. He's nowhere to be seen, but the shower turns on in the bathroom.

He slept on the floor. For me.

Sitting up, I'm still swimming in Keegan's prep school t-shirt he gave me last night after I got out of the bath. I dip my nose into the fabric and breathe in deep. Hints of his laundry detergent filter through my senses. The last time Keegan and I spent the night together, we were in sleeping bags and told scary stories until I was so frightened I slept with a flashlight in my hand, darting the beam around the room to illuminate all the shadows my eyes tricked me into seeing.

This feels so much different. So much *better*.

The bathroom door opens a little while later. Keegan steps through with a pair of low-slung joggers hugging his hips. Ripped, muscled abs ripple as he runs a towel over his wet hair. I force my lips together to keep from drooling and making a fool out of myself.

After shaking his hair out, he peers over at me. "Your dad's been blowing up your phone. He wants to know if you're okay. I wrote him and told him you were sleeping."

I bring my legs to my chest and nod groggily. My head feels like it weighs double what it usually does, but the image of Keegan in front of me makes me want to come around sooner.

Moving to his closet, he searches through his shirts. I frown as he pulls one off the hanger and puts it on while his back is turned. With one hand on the closet door, he says, "I hate that that happened to you last night. All because of me."

My tongue feels like sandpaper, but I force the words out anyway. "Because of you?"

"If I hadn't let it slip in front of Anne-Marie that you were a virgin, no one would know. I was just so—" He growls, the sound low in this throat.

"You can talk to me," I urge. I've been wanting to know what makes Keegan Forbes tick for a long time. It certainly isn't just sex and money. It can't be. I wouldn't have fallen so hard for someone like that.

Spinning toward me, he pins me with a hard glare. He takes me in, and little by little, his features soften. I have his shirt pulled around my legs, my chin resting atop my knees. He flexes his fingers. "You don't know what it's like to be me, Delilah." He pushes off the closet door and stalks closer. "The further I got from you, the more it became abundantly clear that you and I were never going to happen. If I couldn't have you, I wanted to make sure no one else could either. Mistakenly, I thought being a virgin would embarrass you and turn off all of the guys in this school. But that's where I screwed up. I forgot about the chase, the drive to take something that's not yours.

You've been mine for so long that no one would look at you twice because they knew I'd do something about it. The moment—" He leans over me, jaw locked tight. "The moment I let it slip that I hadn't gone there with you, they all came out. They thought they had a chance because I hadn't laid my claim. Some of these pigs believe it's okay to think about you now. Probably daydreaming about having your perfect thighs wrapped around their neck."

"Stop, Keegan," I warn as his anger rises. He's only reminding me of the stalkerish gift I received last night.

"I had to show them you still weren't available. C—"

"Cameron, I know," I finish for him. I already saw his black eye.

"No, café guy," Keegan grinds out.

I suck in a breath. Keegan jumped Tim? Keegan Forbes? To my knowledge, he's never jumped anyone in his life. "You didn't..."

"I see the way he looks at you ever since you paid attention to him that day. He watches you. He smiles when you smile. I needed to send him a message."

I gulp. "And Cameron?"

"Devon told me what he said. He had to be taught a lesson for himself and for all the other sick psychos out there who now want a piece of you. We live in a land of wolves."

"And you made me the injured, bleeding animal, Keegan."

"No, I made you the prize."

I shake my head, and he follows too. "I'll kill them if they touch you. I'll eviscerate whoever sent you that sick bouquet. You're mine, Delilah Astor. I don't care if I deserve you or not. I don't even care if you can't stand me right now. I'm not going to sit back any longer."

"Sitting back?" I narrow my gaze. "Keegan, you act as if you've been an innocent bystander. You cheated on me. You continued to show up to functions with other girls, showing me every damn time that you obviously weren't waiting around for me, so stop fooling yourself that you were."

"I was sick of never being enough for you. Everything I did, you scrutinized until you made me the enemy. I'm not going to be your savior, Dee. It's not in me."

I reach out, sliding my fingers over his. "Then what was last night?"

His jaw feathers.

"You came to my rescue when I called you. You were right here, ready to fight for me."

"Because you needed me. You never need me, Dee. You're so strong."

"That doesn't mean I don't need people. You think I want to be strong all the time? You think I want to go around acting like things don't bother me when they do? Keegan, I have to be one of the wolves or I'll get eaten alive faster than anyone else. When people see women in our circle, they see weakness. If I'm not an in-their-face, smart, quick-thinking bitch, they'll walk all over me. I can't let that happen."

He sits on the bed, elbows on his knees as he runs his hands through his thick hair. "I want to take care of you."

"I want that too. But I don't need someone who's going to make every decision for me and work while I stay home. That's not who I am. I just need a partner, Keegan. I'm not trying to emasculate you, and I don't want you to pigeonhole me into a stay-at-home-mom who day drinks and hooks up with the pool boy. I want a fucking fighter at my side."

He peeks over at me, the gray shirt he pulled on taut over his shoulders. His blue eyes dance with lust. "Do you remember the first time I kissed you? You told me I was doing it wrong."

I snicker. "Only because my entire knowledge of kissing at the time was seeing my mother and father peck on the lips, and you were trying to suck my lips off my face."

His cheeks bloom an angry red, and my stomach sours. I'd meant it as a light-hearted comment, but something I've said has gotten to him.

He turns away. "I've seen things I shouldn't. A lot of things." His Adam's apple bobs before he stares right back at me. "I only knew that I wanted to be as close to you as possible. I always have, Dee."

Heat pools between my legs. I straighten them on the bed, squeezing them together. The shirt pulls up over my thighs. I don't have to look down to know that my nipples are peaking right through his thin shirt.

Since he wants to be close to me, I think we can make that happen. "How about now?" I ask, drifting my knees apart. The shirt travels up and up until it's around my hips, my bare pussy on display.

He doesn't even drop his gaze. He crawls forward, moving his hand up my thigh until the shirt tangles in his grip. He brings it up, dropping a kiss above my belly button, then my upper torso. "I've been wanting to see you shirtless since the wet t-shirt contest. I know that makes me a horny bastard, but I am one when it comes to you." He moves the material to the swell of my breasts before hesitating. "Can I take this off?"

Maybe Keegan and I can meet in the middle. He can restrain his baser instincts, and I can relax a little. I'll give him more power as long as he doesn't suck me dry. And he can show me he cares by doing things like this—by asking permission. Nodding, I lean forward to raise my hands in the air. He pulls the soft shirt over my head, past my hands, and throws it to the side. I'm naked in front of his fully clothed body. I'm baring all of my vulnerabilities to him, but it doesn't feel wrong because he's just bared his to me.

Reaching out with both hands, he cups my breasts. I push my chest forward, making him take all of them as they spill into his hands. "These got bigger," he notes on a prayer-like whisper. He slides his thumbs over my hard nipples, forcing them to tighten under his attention. "I don't deserve you."

I lean back on my hands, and he follows forward.

"That's where you're wrong. I just wanted you to work for it."

He massages my breasts, plucking and caressing until I'm squeezing my thighs together to keep from leaking all over his bed. "I want to see," Keegan purrs, forcing my legs open. In my heightened state of arousal, even the air passing over my sensitive flesh makes me moan.

"Mmmm," he rumbles. "Look at that perfect pussy."

My core tightens at his words, and I whimper in the back of my throat.

Moving forward, he presses a chaste kiss to my neck while stroking my breasts. "Touch yourself," Keegan hisses. "I want to watch."

I start to move my hands up under his to cup my mounds but he shakes his head.

"Your pussy, sweet Delilah. I have this handled. I want you to make yourself come all over your fingers."

"Keegan..."

I press my lips together as he pinches my nipples to cut me off. "Show me how you do it when you're thinking of me."

That, I know about. I sneak my fingers down my front, over my mound, and to my core. Dipping my fingers into the pleasure I've leaked, I move up to my clit, circling the pad of my finger over the tiny nub. My body responds immediately, my hips bucking toward him.

"Jesus," he breathes.

He watches me for a few moments before surging forward to take one of my nipples into his hot mouth. I cry out, quickening my speed over my clit. "Keegan, oh my God." The moan that follows is raw, an unhindered response to the pleasure coursing through me.

"Baby, that's fucking hot. Keep going," he murmurs, his lips still moving over my flesh.

As if I could stop. My hips move upward, as if they want to search him out. I tighten my circle, rubbing furiously as he pulls away. My breaths heave out in uneven bursts of air interspersed with cries of excitement. I'm already getting so close. His caresses, the pure naughtiness of having him watch me. I'm barreling forward. "Keegan," I cry out as I sail over the edge without a parachute. Pressing my eyes closed, I keep my fingers on my center as I come apart, my core muscles tightening and releasing in a flurry of contractions.

As the high wears off, my muscles relax. With it comes Keegan's soothing voice. "Open your eyes, beautiful girl."

I press my lips into a thin line to buy me some time. Breathing out, I flutter my eyes open and stare into the gaze of the man I always thought Keegan could be.

Something's changed in him. Switched. Maybe it's because he understands me better, and I him. Maybe it's because he's unabashedly sexy staring at me with his pouty mouth as my body decides to squeeze one last time.

I moan, moving my fingers away, and grab him behind the neck, forcing his lips to mine. As insignificant as this moment might be to others, Keegan and I have just had a breakthrough. He let me take control, taking the reins while he watched. He understood what I needed from him in a moment like this. And kissing him, forcing my tongue past his lips, I try to infuse in him that I'll work with him, too. I can let my guard down around him. Of all people, it should be him.

He pulls away, searing his gaze into mine. "I've never let anything happen to you, Dee, and I won't start now. We'll find out who sent you that, and we'll make them pay."

As things shift into place, I can breathe easier than I have in years. Keegan and I were always meant to be weathering the hardships of this life together, and finally—finally—it feels like I can look forward again.

15

I sit next to Keegan on the couch cushions. The smell of coffee envelops me as he places his arm around my shoulders. Devon sits on the opposite couch with his arms folded over his chest, eyeing the two of us.

Something feels different with Keegan this time. Then again, we were always happy in the beginning. It's only been twenty-four hours, so I should probably lower my expectations, but I've never been one to do that when it came to our relationship. I'm all in, and if the fall happens, I'll suffer the consequences just as I have in the past.

I got off the phone with my dad a little while ago. The lab he sent the semen sample to said it was corrupted with bleach. So, not only did the asshole jerk off to my picture, but he covered it up too. No fingerprints were found on any of the items, but they're still running tests.

I don't know what I expected. If the guy who did this is anything like us, he would know enough not to leave evidence behind. We can't even get anything off the picture. The tabloid I was in had come out that morning, so anyone could've gotten their hands on it.

"I LIKE THIS," DEVON SAYS, NODDING.

He takes me away from my thoughts, and I smile at him. "Yeah, Keegan finally pulled his head out of his ass," I tease.

Keegan tenses, but he releases it in the next breath. "About time," Devon praises. "You guys were always perfect for each other. Plus, this will keep the vultures away."

He doesn't even know the half of it. I've been walking around campus with my head on a swivel. Thankfully, Keegan has been escorting me everywhere like I've hired him to be my own personal bodyguard.

Nothing like a stalkerish gift to bring two people together, I suppose.

Luckily, since I had my father on the phone, I could also ask him about previous Devil's Night parties since he'd yet to respond to my email. Sure, I threw a more urgent matter into his hands, but that doesn't mean I can slack off on a job.

As expected, it sounds like the epitome of male arousal and exploitation of wealth. My father relayed the information to me in business-like terms. Hearing him call half-naked women 'beautiful, nude models' was something I don't wish to have repeated again. Especially since the women we have coming are my age. Honestly, if I think about it too long, it makes me want to puke.

We leave Devon with unanswered questions as to how we finally got together. Neither one of us wants to rehash it, but our Knights meeting is a ready excuse to leave the café. We walk to the KOA shoulder-to-shoulder. The usual suspects watch us. Like with multimillion dollar businesses, every movement from challenging parties can mean something. Right now, we're big news.

My gaze darts to the men on campus, wondering if they're the ones who sent the bouquet, and even further, if they actually thought that was something that I'd be into or if they meant for it to be scary as hell.

"Delilah?"

I turn at the sound of the husky voice. Tim's leaning against the back of the café building again, an apron securely fastened around his waist. "Oh hey," I wave, acutely aware of the body who hasn't left my side, and the knowledge that he's actually the one who hurt Tim, leaving the currently yellowing bruises on his face.

"I didn't see you this morning."

I blush at the memory of what Keegan and I were doing this morning after spending the night in his bed together. We haven't taken it all the way yet, but I'm dying to. I was always saving it for him, and as soon as I know he's not going to turn right around and leave me, I'm ready to give it to him. "Woke up late."

I doubt he even hears my explanation because Keegan talks over me. "She was in good hands. You don't have to worry." Jesus. Testosterone flows off both of them in tidal waves that could drown an elite swimmer.

I elbow Keegan. He and I haven't talked about what he did to Tim, but we will be soon. "See you around," I call out, turning away before Keegan decides he wants to show the café barista that he can't have me. When we're far enough away, I sigh. "You didn't have to do that. And you really didn't have to beat him up."

"He likes you," he grinds out. "We should have your dad look into him."

"Tim?" I gasp. "No way. He's just a local."

Keegan's lips thin. "I'm so glad you're on a first name basis with the barista."

I smile over at him. "I wouldn't be if you hadn't acted like a dick."

He pushes his tongue against his teeth and peers straight ahead.

"Oh, come on," I chastise. "You deserved that one."

Pulling me to a stop, he threads his arm around my hips and tugs me close. "Promise me you'll forget his name." Dipping lower, he whispers into my ear. "I can fuck it out of you."

Butterflies take flight in my chest. "I'm actually quite intelligent. I don't think I could just forget his name."

His lips press together, but then he grins, mouth widening as time goes by. The stress, the need to be in control, falters. "You are smart, Dee. I wouldn't want it any other way." He reaches up to play with the ends of my hair. "Just remember wolves can come in sheep's clothing, too. We can't be too careful."

I understand where he's coming from, however, Tim is neither a sheep nor a wolf. He knows nothing about the world I'm in. All he sees is the surface of it, the jerks who bark out their orders callously. However, our world goes much deeper than that.

"Let's just focus on the meeting," I tell Keegan. "Dad's handling the other stuff, and despite how awful this party is going to be, it's tradition."

"That's the spirit," he cajoles.

When he starts to walk away, I hold back on his arm. "Oh, I just want to say, if you show up to the party with another girl or disappear down a hallway with one of our lovely wet t-shirt contest winners, there will never be an us again. Understand?"

He swallows, all teasing leaving him. "I completely and utterly understand. That's not going to happen."

I almost take a step back from the force of his words. Instead, I give him a quick nod, and we continue toward the Knights building.

Stepping inside, we make our way to the meeting room. Everyone else is already there as we take our spots. Cameron rolls his eyes. "Awesome. The destined king and queen are back together."

I ignore him, and instead of retaliating, Keegan starts the meeting. "I contacted Mrs. Dupont, an event organizer, to plan the party. She's waiting on our orders. Now, what did we find out?"

We go around the room, discussing what we found out from our fathers and then giving our best ideas to be mulled over and decided on between the committee members. In the end, my theme wins. We're having a devil/angel party for Devil's Night, which, surprisingly, we could not find evidence of in the past. Formal attire has always been required, but this party will be more of a theme, even complete with costumes. Face masks were Keegan's suggestion. He pinched my thigh under the table when he mentioned it, and I was thrown back to the sorority contest for one hot moment.

The winners from the competition were chosen and contacted, except for one girl who wasn't wearing a number. Keegan bordered on being furious that the secret girl got enough votes, and at the same time, he bursted with pride, a feeling I noted when his heavy gaze slid to mine.

At this point, I may burst from all of our heated glances and lingering stares.

Next, we move on to activities, gifts, games, and prizes. At the end of two hours, we have the basis of our Devil's Night Party. Even I get into its planning even though I would rather gouge my eyes out with a spoon than attend.

Not attending really isn't an option for me, though. The amount of money this will cost is obscene. The gifts alone are pricey as hell, even though it's to be expected. What do you get for people who buy anything and everything they want?

The nude models, who—thanks to me—won't be winging it in their birthday suit, are also getting gift bags that will probably pay their next year's tuition in full. I pushed for more, and the guys were willing to concede, most likely for their own nefarious reasons, but I'm choosing not to get spun around in that hamster wheel.

At the conclusion, all of our tasks moving forward are divvied up. I'm not stressing that the other members won't get their work done because all of our standings as Knights hinge on this. Cameron will come up with the hide and seek treasure hunt trail to get our guests to the island. Reginald Wright's son will be the liaison between us and the event planner. As for myself, I'm the go-between for the girls. I'm planning their costumes and their goodie bags, and I'll also be around to make sure no one does anything to them that they don't want to do.

With just under two weeks left, there is so much yet to be done.

Keegan pulls Wright aside just before we leave, giving him Mrs. Dupont's information. She's planned parties for mine and Keegan's families multiple times. We know she'll get the job done right and to our specs.

Heavy musk fills my nostrils. I glance up as I make notes, and Cameron smirks down at me. "You made the wrong choice."

I sigh. "For what, Cabot?"

He shifts his gaze to Keegan. I look that way, too, watching as a focused Keegan gives instructions like he's standing in front of a line of important people. His shoulders are rigid, his brows move as he listens to

Wright respond. I can't hear what they're saying, but I've been watching Keegan for so long that I know he thinks Wright's an imbecile. Then again, he thinks a lot of people are imbeciles.

Hot breath hits my cheek. "You know what they say, once a cheater, always a cheater."

The hairs on the back of my neck rise. I whip around to face Cameron and stand, forcing him to give me space. "Like you care. You only wanted one thing out of your offer."

"And you think he wants more?" His sinister laugh shakes the steel in my spine. He's hitting all the anxious parts of me. "Hopefully he pops that cherry before someone else just takes it, Delilah."

The warning rolls off his tongue like ice. Could Cameron be the asshole who left me that disgusting, twisted gift?

As soon as I think it, I remind myself that Keegan and I were the first to leave the bar last night. Cameron and the rest of the guys in this room were still partying. There wasn't enough time for him to leave the bar, beat me to my room, and disappear before Keegan left me. Right?

Leaving me with a pit in my stomach, Cameron exits the room just as Keegan finishes his conversation with Wright. The cave-like room feels cold and damp as dread creeps into my body again.

"You okay?" Keegan asks.

I nod, telling myself that it's fine. Cameron's just an ass. He's pouting because he really thought a self-respecting woman would take him up on his ridiculous offer. The only thing he's guilty of is being delusional.

Footsteps echo through the hallway. Keegan and I glance up as Reginald Wright blocks our way out of the room. "Fledglings. I've been meaning to ask how Miss Astor is doing?"

He peers at Keegan as if he's the only one who can give him a truthful answer. Before I can fall down the rabbit hole of how many times Keegan has betrayed me since we returned from break, the devil himself speaks up. "Yes, Sir. We were actually just at our Devil's Night Party meeting. I assure you her invaluable suggestions are going to make the best Devil's Night Party yet."

Sir Wright looks me up and down, stare lingering until I start to shift on my feet. "Has she now?"

"I'm sure all the elders will be pleasantly surprised with what we have in the works."

"Excellent, Mr. Forbes," he praises, except he's not looking at Keegan at all, he's staring at me as if he can see straight through my clothes, practically undressing me with his eyes. It feels as if I'm walking through spiderwebs.

"Ready?" I ask Keegan, eager to get the hell out of here.

Keegan gestures toward the door, and I take off after quickly grabbing my notes and shoving them in my bag. The red alert feeling doesn't leave until I escape the walls of the Knights lair.

16

A week and a half passes, and I barely have time to breathe. Between keeping up with my studies, making sure the Devil's Night party will go off without a hitch, and sticking to the shadows so I go unnoticed, it's all becoming too much.

I'm used to being in the spotlight for good things, but the rumor about me still being a virgin has spread all around campus, making me the number one person to gawk at. They're always ribbing each other, jutting their chins out toward me as if I can't see them. They whisper behind their hands. I've even had other ladies approach me, telling me they think it's honorable I've kept it all this time.

Honestly, I don't know what to do with that. I wasn't doing it as some sort of purity test for myself. In fact, I can't wait to give it away to Keegan. We spend the night in either my room or his. Nothing else has happened. No freaky flowers with semen-filled condoms, just lingering looks from most of campus. It's difficult to pinpoint any weird behavior because it's all strange.

Three days ago, Keegan shouted at everyone in the café to get a fucking life because I felt like I was the subject in a lab test. He stormed from the building, telling Devon to watch me as he blew off some steam in the gym.

He's taking this all on himself, but honestly, even I didn't realize how big this was going to be. I kind of want to fake another rumor just to take the onus off me and place it on someone else.

Campus is littered with dead leaves as Halloween approaches. The holiday has taken a little of the attention off me because everyone is talking about the upcoming parties. But, as far as I know, the Knights are the only one planning the most epic bash of the year. No one else on the CU campus even knows what Devil's Night is apparently. Or cares.

Night of Mischief my ass. The Knights should call it, Night of Spending Entirely Too Much Money In Absolutely Frivolous Ways.

I really have been spending too much time listening to Eden.

Dad and I are keeping her in the dark about what

happened. If it's a one-off incident, we're not going to worry either her or my mother about it. Everything came back clean with no evidence, and with the way I'm suddenly so popular, I wouldn't be surprised if someone did it as a sick prank. The son or daughter of a family rival? All the families who attend CU have been screwed over by other families here. Someone who believes I did them wrong? Hell, I've even pegged it on Anne-Marie because it's obvious she likes Keegan. She could've had sex with a guy, stolen the condom, and threw it in the bouquet. She's diabolical like that. I bet she wishes she had never even spread the rumor, considering all the attention it's gotten me.

If life were fair, she'd be next in line. However, she'd preen with all the extra eyes on her.

The secret *Devil & Angel Party* invitations went out yesterday. After discussing the guest list with the other committee members, I wasn't lucky enough to have her excluded. Her father is a Knight. He was just one who didn't want his daughter to join.

The deeper I get into the Knight culture, the more my faith wavers. Changing a group that's been around for centuries is an insurmountable task. It doesn't feel like I'm doing all that much. I got the girls to actually wear white lingerie instead of being naked. So what? There won't be a sex dungeon in the castle. Who cares? These are just basic things that should've been put into place a long time ago. I'm fighting against a huge brick wall that was shored up a long time ago. Is this even something I have a chance of winning against? Or am I just spinning my wheels? Dread sets in the nearer we get to the party. Nerves and apprehension skim at the surface all the time.

It feels as if I'm setting myself up for failure.

Keegan massages my shoulders. His fingers work magic into the knots hanging out there. Yesterday, I confessed my worries to him. Don't get me wrong, he's not all on board with me changing the Knights, but he is all on board with me. That's as much as I can ask for right now. "You're thinking about it again," he chastises.

We're in the library, the stark white fluorescent lights overhead making the picture in my head crystal clear. I shrug. "I don't know. I just can't shake the feeling that the party's not a good idea."

He bends, his cheek scratching against mine. "It's a tradition. There's nothing you can do about it."

Despite my best efforts, the girls we chose are all super excited about Devil's Night. I met with them the other day to talk about the timeline of events. They were all giddy with excitement. I could practically see the dollar signs in their eyes as I showed them the costumes they're wearing and brought along the seamstress to take their measurements.

There's power in sex and sexual appeal, but how can I fight against the devaluing of women when I'm made to have this role? When the very girls I'm trying to fight for see nothing wrong with it? "Maybe I worry too much," I admit.

"You have a lifetime to plead your case, Dee." He moves one of the wooden chairs next to me and sits. "You're already changing their minds. Sir Wright hasn't asked me about you again. He's all but forgotten about my complaint. If they like you, they'll open their minds to more women being Knights. With more women comes more change."

I narrow my gaze. He doesn't sound like the Keegan I've known sometimes.

He holds his hands up. "I know. You're calling bullshit. I like the Knights the way they are, you know that. But it means something to you, and you mean something to me." He grabs my hand and strokes my palm with the tips of his fingers. "I'm learning a lot from you and trying to be open-minded. I can see why you feel the way you do." He shrugs. With every little thing he says, he starts to fill the mile-wide pit between us. He doesn't believe in my vision yet, but he sees that I care about it, so I trust him when he says he's trying. I always knew he had the capacity to care inside him. The scope to look past his own needs and desires to see the world through others' eyes.

I lean forward to kiss him. "I know you do," I whisper, thankful to have him back as an ally instead of an enemy. He makes the worst enemy because he knows so much about me it's scary. We've revealed a lot of truths to each other over the last week. He hasn't felt like he was good enough for me in a long time. He delivered a self-fulfilling prophecy by sleeping with other women. Uncertainty got him too. In our world, no one wants a wife who sticks up for herself. Unfortunately—and fortunately—my father taught me the exact opposite. I'm not a "sit in the corner and look pretty" kind of girl, and it takes a strong man to be with someone like me. Given our backgrounds, it's a wonder we're not an epic rivalry in the making, destined to clash over and over again.

"Tomorrow's your second big step," Keegan states.

"Second?"

"The first was making it into the Knights," he whispers, an unsure gaze darting around the recesses of the library. "I never congratulated you like I should have. I was jealous."

"I can't stop being who I am," I tell him. It's the one sticking point I keep having with Keegan. I have a feeling this point of contention will be with us throughout our entire lives.

"And I don't want you to be. I'd rather you be you

than let me win. Plus, you just push me to work harder."

I grin. "That's not all bad then."

"Not at all. Actually, I'd rather lose to you than anyone else."

"Ooh, coming out with the compliments, I see."

His eyes flash. "Nothing but the best for my—" He trails off, cocking his head to the side. "I guess we still have to figure that part out, don't we?"

Nerves flutter in my stomach. Neither one of us knows how to tread this line. I've always loved him. I've always hoped we'd end up on an altar someday. Sure, there's an agreement between our families, but we have to feel it too. I promised myself a long time ago that I wouldn't pressure him. I'd let him travel the course in his own time.

"Is Eden coming to the party?"

I shake my head. "Yeah, right. She's loving life where she is. Her invitation was a formality. There's no way she's leaving her school to slum it with us in jacket weather right now. Besides, you'll probably have to apologize when you see her, and that doesn't sound like something you'll enjoy doing."

He grimaces. "How much does she know about what's been going on?"

"I haven't told her a thing. The less she knows the better. She already thinks I'm crazy for wanting to follow in Dad's footsteps, and the idea of the Devil's Night Party is everything she hates about being an Astor."

"Does she know about me?"

I bite my lip, loving that he actually cares to know. "Not yet," I tell him. "I didn't know how to tell her."

He presses his lips together. "You didn't just come out and tell her that you can't wait to impale yourself on my dick?"

I nearly choke, then squeeze his hand to chastise him. "I definitely did not say that."

"You should tell her because it's true."

"You wish, Keegan Forbes."

"Your constantly drenched panties say otherwise, Beautiful Girl."

"Why haven't you just done it?" I ask, mirroring a question I've asked him before. This time, we're in different places though. I'm willing to give it to him. "You haven't asked."

He licks his lips. "I'm waiting for the perfect time." Sitting up, he stretches and then closes his textbook that he barely looked at the entire time we were here.

"When will that be?"

"You'll see," he tells me. "In the meantime, we'll just have to keep experimenting with different ways to get each other off."

He has that look in his eyes. It heats me up from

the inside out until I find myself throwing my textbook in my bag and standing.

"You're always surprising me, Delilah," he rasps out. He threads his fingers through mine, and we make our way out of the library. He turns me in the direction of my room, which is the closest to where we are right now.

We practically run around the side of the building, and I walk smack into an impenetrable barrier. Keegan keeps me from falling. "The fuck," he growls.

I blink to find Tim reaching out to help steady me on my feet.

"Get your hands off her."

Tim listens, his hand falling away. It brushes my pants pocket on the way down. "It's okay," I tell Keegan. "I'm fine. Sorry, Tim. We didn't see you."

"Are you okay?" he asks.

"It's nothing," I say, laughing humorlessly. The back of my neck heats in embarrassment. Tim and Keegan stare at each other like they'd gladly take the others' head off if provoked. I push Keegan ahead, figuring it's best to get him out of the situation. I turn, waving to Tim as we leave.

He deliberately drops his gaze to my pocket. Keegan curses under his breath, but luckily, he keeps striding toward my building. I press my hand to my jeans and feel the edge of a piece of paper sticking out.

I don't know why Tim is passing me a note, but I don't want to alert Keegan to it either. He'll just blow it out of proportion. I stick it fully back inside my pocket and take Keegan's arm, rubbing my hand up and down it to soothe him.

The note feels like a lead weight as I absentmindedly walk across campus, stepping on fallen leaves. I turn my head around again to peek back at Tim. He's still watching, his arms crossed over his chest.

Facing front again, I peer straight ahead, shaking off the unnerving feeling as best I can. Was that anger in his eyes?

"You sure you're okay?" Keegan asks.

"Totally fine," I lie.

Totally fine.

eegan parks his sports car at the dock. We're a far cry from the Mediterranean, but the St. Lawrence River is pretty enough. Winding through small villages and larger tourist towns, the variety of structures found on its banks is astounding. Normal sized houses give way to huge mansions with sea walls and slides that end right in the river. I've been lucky enough to stay in fancy places around the world, but some of the most opulent homes are ones I've seen here.

Our forefathers vacationed here. The richest men in the world came to this very area to escape busy lives. Old money. New money. Men who built their wives castles because they could.

As for the Knights of Arcadia, we're the proud owners of our own immaculate castle on Dark Island.

My gaze settles on the boat we've hired to take us down river. My stomach bottoms out. I love boating, but I'll never forget the way the water clogged my lungs when I was little. In small vessels like the one I'm staring at, the water is closer, more alive. It'll dip and bob with the wakes of other boats and jet skis. Fear starts to crawl up my spine.

A striking yellow jet ski flies by just in front of us, motor gunning. Water sprays out the back in a rushing fountain. I frown at the scene, and Keegan gives me a pat on the hand. "It'll be over in no time. It's only a half an hour to the island."

Luckily.

Keegan's explained to me in-depth of what to expect. I'm excited to see a real-life castle, but the journey to get there? Not so much.

Our guests, if they succeed in their treasure hunt, will find themselves at this very dock where captains we've hired will transport them down the seaway, dropping them off at our castle for a night of privileged fun.

Today, though, this is where us committee members head to the island to make sure everything is coming together smoothly. Mrs. Dupont has already been at the island for a few days. Since she has to get everything carried over by boat, it's a hassle coordinating everything.

Keegan gets out of his car and grabs our bags from

the back. Other committee members arrive. We move out onto the dock as a collective group where an old fisherman waits. His gray hair curls out around his hat as he waves us on board. Keegan helps me down into the boat, and I find a seat in the middle, clasping the seat securely. Despite the rough-around-the-edges look of the captain, the small dingy we're taking over is nice and updated.

The other committee members chat happily about the upcoming days. We've put all the work into this party that we could. Now it's just time for us to cross our fingers and hope everything goes off without a hitch and that the elders are pleasantly surprised with what we've done to celebrate Devil's Night with them.

The sun warms my thighs as I peer out over the water. The weather is unseasonably warm today for this part of the country. The guy on the jet ski was still wearing a wet suit, but the fact that he even braved the water on something you're bound to get wet on says something.

Cameron shields his eyes from the bright rays and points the opposite way the boat takes us. "My dad bought a house down there a couple of years ago. It's fun to come here, but it's not all that exciting. I bet the yearly Devil's Night party at the Knights Castle is the only thing to liven the area up."

The "house" that he's talking about probably boasts

more than ten bedrooms and has more finery than most people can imagine. My great grandfather owned a house on the St. Lawrence until my grandfather sold it. My father, who had great memories of visiting the place when he was a child, had always wanted to purchase it back, but the current people who own it aren't selling.

As we motor down the river, the captain points out different islands and the structures that stand on it. There's a reason why this place is called the Thousand Islands region. Islands of all shapes and sizes dot the river, some as small as to only boast a one-room house with front steps that lead down into the water. For the bigger places, his list is a who's who of rich families as he spouts their names. Most of the guys aren't paying attention, but I watch as he deftly maneuvers the vessel around the river like a pro and narrates. When he turns toward me, his hat has an insignia on it for a local boat tour company.

"What can you tell me about the place you're taking us to?" I ask. I don't say anything about the Knights, of course, but I'm interested in what other people think the place is.

He looks down his nose at me. "I know once a year a bunch of stuffy, rich-looking people like yourselves need someone to captain their asses down the river, so I do."

His gruff response makes me press my lips together, so I don't laugh. He's hit the nail on the head, actually. And, if he does this every year, I wouldn't be surprised if we're paying him for his secrecy.

Keegan drops his arm around my shoulders and cuddles closer. "You're making friends everywhere, Dee."

"I guess it's my charm."

The captain continues his monotone explanation of houses and backstories. It's clear he doesn't care if we listen or not. He could even be spouting facts off on autopilot. I'm sure a tour wasn't necessarily in the agreement we have with him.

Minutes later, Keegan squeezes my arm and juts his chin toward the aft side of the boat. I peer over, watching in awe as a legit castle moves into view. From our position in the water, I spot a formidable wall rising into the air, a boat house that's big enough for three covered slips, and a small turret. The island it sits on is large. Half of it filled with trees and uninhabited, but the other boasts beautiful, manicured grounds. "Wow."

"Yeah, it's beautiful, isn't it?"

I don't have any words as we get close enough to really pick out the structure's details. Weathered, dark gray stones make up the exterior. A red, shingle roof accents the many different roof lines. Six stories tall, some of the castle's levels are sunk into the hillside while others rise above it. It's as if the island grew around the castle instead of vice versa.

The captain docks the boat and a bevy of servants surround us to take our things. Dressed smartly in crisp red, bellhop appropriate uniforms, they tell us our room's location as we give them our names. I'm positively enamored with the whole process. Here, I've stepped back into the early 1900's. I wish I'd chosen a different dress to wear tonight. Maybe something with a corset and a big skirt to complete the ambiance surrounding me.

We follow the servants up the curving stone walk. Ahead of us, the entrance is understated and in complete contrast to the luxury around us. The wooden door is intricate enough, but it's small compared to the grandiosity of the rest of the structure.

Stone floors greet us in the small foyer. Furniture and decoration are everywhere. A legit suit of armor stands against one wall. To the left, a sign next to an open staircase states the Wine Cellar is downstairs.

Quickly moving past, we step up into an enormous room that throws me back in time even more. Huge, dark cherry furniture, beautiful glass chandeliers, and wood floors are polished like new. A grand staircase slopes upward directly in front of us, and a man with a tuxedo waits on the bottom step to announce that our rooms are upstairs if we'd like to get settled. He then introduces himself as the castle butler who would be happy to take care of any of our needs during our stay.

Keegan threads his fingers through mine, and I look to the right and left as we make our way toward the stairs. Everywhere I look, workers are busying themselves with cleaning and decorating. Mrs. Dupont, a wisp thin woman with a severe ponytail, points bodies in each direction as she spouts orders. I grin at Keegan. "This is going to be fun."

His eyes hood. "I'm happy to hear you say that."

A stay in this place alone will be worth the price I'll have to pay to put up with the no-holds-barred, dreams-come-true scenario we're setting up for the Knight elders and our guests. No mischief needed, but I'm sure there will be some. There always is when you get a bunch of high-powered, money-wielding men in a room together.

We traipse up three flights of stairs to find a grand hall lined with bedrooms. Names hang outside each one, so it's easy to pick our assigned bedroom. Luckily, Keegan and I are right next to each other, but we won't be needing separate rooms.

He follows me past the doorway that has my name on it. The room widens into a huge space, complete with a four-poster bed and intricate box seats in front of the windows. The only other door in the room leads to an immaculate en suite. Turning around in the space to take it all in, I spot huge, deep cherry wardrobes flanking the door to the hallway. I pull on the antique knobs to find empty hangers and an iron with ironing board.

"I think I can get used to this," Keegan says, looking upward at the high ceilings.

I follow his gaze. No detail was spared. "I have a new goal," I tell him.

"Castle?"

"Mm-hmm. It's a fairytale."

He grins. "We'll just have to make that happen then." Moving closer, he slides his arm around my back, pulling me against him. "What do you say? Chateau Forbes?"

My lips tease into a smile. "Astor has a better ring to it, but I'll take what I can get."

He snickers, playfully pinching my skin. "Fine. How about Astor Castle on Forbes Island?"

I turn into him and press up onto my toes to give him a quick kiss on the cheek before whispering, "I think you may have something there."

"I think I'll like having you on top of me for all of time. You, the castle. Me, the island."

I shake my head at his horrible sexual innuendo. "That was bad."

His chest shakes with his laughter. "Yeah, but I mean it." With a quick kiss to my forehead, he steps back. "I'm going to get settled. Meet you in a bit to tour and make sure everything is on track for tomorrow?"

"Sure," I tell him. I'm practically shaking with eager anticipation to see what the rest of the freaking castle looks like, but I also know we're here to do a job. I won't be coming back to this place if we don't get a favorable review on the party, so that needs to be my number one concern.

I hang up my dress for tomorrow, and also place the shoes I bought just for the occasion in the wardrobe, and then shove my bag inside too. Next, I check out the bed. It's a west-facing window, so the sun streams in through the glass panes, lighting up the interior of the room and making the ivory satin of the comforter appear even more inviting. An old grandfather clock sits on the mantle above the fireplace. No fire needed today, however, it looks to be a working showpiece. A set of black, iron fireplace tools sit next to it along with a gold pail that's used to hold ashes.

I flop back on the bed, staring at the intricate, sunburst pattern that flares out toward the edges of the wall and away from the hanging, glass chandelier. I've been in plenty of beautiful houses, but none have had quite the pomp that this one does. The amount of money this took to build originally must have been astronomical.

"Dude," I hear out in the hallway. "This place is amazing!"

I get up from the bed and stick my head out to find a few of the committee guys walking toward the stairs. I shout after them. "We should all meet downstairs to make sure everything is coming along."

"Yep, see you down there, Dee."

I close my door and walk toward Keegan's room. Before I can even get there, he steps out. "Ready?"

I step back as he intertwines our fingers. "Ready."

"Let's go, guys," Keegan yells, staring into open rooms. "Meeting downstairs, five minutes. Let's work, and then we'll play." He gives me a wink, and we head down the staircase. This time, I run my hand down the ornate, curved railing.

Mrs. Dupont meets us at the bottom. "Proceed to the garden room, and I'll give you an update."

She points toward an area that to get to, you have to move through two different living areas and a library. There's not enough time for me to see everything, but I promise myself I'll take a more in-depth tour myself at some point while I'm here. In the garden area, the large, round tables interspersed throughout the space make it evident this will be where our meal will be served. Dark red tablecloths adorn each table, complete with chair covers and hors d'oeuvre stands. But that's not what catches my eye the most. This room is lined with arched windows on three sides. The ceiling goes up another floor where square windows adorn the top along with skylights that let light pour into the room. If the walls weren't stone, you could trick yourself into thinking you weren't in a castle, but instead, in some opulent garden sanctuary.

To our right, servants exit out swinging doors that lead onto a patio that spans the length of the enormous room. Beyond that is the most picturesque view of the river. It could be sold on postcards with how stunning it is, especially with the late afternoon colors streaming through the clouds. No wonder why the Knights own this place and use it for parties. It's grand and stunning, showboating to the world everything they wish to portray: Power, wealth, and prestige.

For the first time in a long time since I joined the Knights, a sense of pride fills me. This place is a stark reminder of the men who came before me. The tradition lining these halls is so overwhelming. I could spend all day walking the rooms and corridors, finding new things and wishing I knew its story.

I'm sure if these walls could talk, they'd have a lot to say.

18

Many times throughout my life, I've considered myself lucky. I grew up privileged. I grew up with niceties some people only dream of. Some as big as yachts, others as small as having the heat turned on during winter. I've never taken what I have for granted, and I've done everything in my power to deserve the life I have, not sitting back and taking it just because my daddy has money. I want to *earn* it.

Quite honestly, there's nothing like walking the halls of a castle to make one feel drunk with power and riches. I'm high off of it. The fact that I get to do this is beyond comprehension.

After eating dinner in a dining room complete with a hidden, hinged wall so servants can sneak in and out, the other Fledglings and myself explore the island.

Darren Greene sprints toward the retaining wall, diving into the river in a sleek line. When he surfaces, he shouts with uninhibited glee. "Fuck that's cold!" Others follow but seeing as how water tried to kill me before, I stick to land. I find a few Adirondack chairs that circle a firepit. With my back toward the forest and the stunning castle as the view in front of me, I've never felt so full of everything a life like mine has to offer.

I pull out my phone and snap a pic. Even if Eden hates everything about our lives, she'll appreciate this. Our favorite pastime when we were kids was pretending we were princesses. We had all the costumes and tiaras to make it easier to make believe, too. I caption the photo with **Don't ask**, then hit Send.

Keegan sits in a chair next to mine. His posh good looks appear more refined with the silhouette of a castle in my same line of sight. "Tomorrow's going to go great," he crows. Turning a smile toward me, he adds, "Thanks to you."

"You too," I tell him. It's obvious the two of us are the ones who put in the extra work. Sure, some of it was us jockeying to take lead, but everything got done.

As the sun starts to set, the servants disappear. Just past where a few of the guys are braving the cold to swim, a whole horde of bodies in the same uniform pile onto a boat and motor away. I wonder how many servants stay overnight. Probably more than usual since we're here. It wouldn't surprise me if this castle is usually only inhabited by the caretaker when one of the Knights isn't visiting.

When stars start to dot the sky, Keegan helps start a fire. Flames leap upward, crackling toward the few clouds lingering high above us. When he comes back to sit, he holds out his hand. I narrow my gaze at it before trusting him. He pulls me to my feet, takes my seat, then tugs me onto his lap where he wraps his arm around me.

Safe and cocooned in his embrace, everything feels too right. He snakes his hand under my shirt, fingers splaying over my back where he traces lines into my skin. I place my head on his shoulder, truly content. As if we're all transfixed by the fire and the setting, none of us speak. It's hard to make true friends because we're taught to be constantly in competition. Even from when we were kids, our parents talked about so-and-so's daughter who graduated with honors while staring at us as if they could will the same thing to happen to us. The saying "It's lonely at the top" is so true. You leave friends behind. You step on their toes until you become rivals. In this world, we do whatever it takes to make it to the next echelon, damn anyone who gets in our way.

Keegan has been with me the longest. Sure, our fathers are rivals, but they're one of the rare few who haven't let their goals in business get in the way of their friendship. They don't take things personally. Some of the guys I'm sitting with around this fire will hate me when we get older. That's okay. If they do, it probably means I'm doing something right.

Our world is cutthroat. With Keegan at my side, things will be much easier.

His fingertips dip underneath the top of my jeans, sliding down to caress the skin there. I peek at him, eyelids heavy. From the look in his eyes, I can tell he wants to kiss me, but we don't dare show that much vulnerability in front of the others.

He leans toward my ear and whispers, "Tell them you're going to bed. Meet me inside."

I bite my lower lip at his demand. Sometimes it's nice being told what to do. It keeps me from having my brain on twenty-four-seven.

Sitting up, I stretch. "I have an early day with the models tomorrow," I announce.

"You mean the hot bitches?" Darren mocks. "I'm going to have one bent over my bed tomorrow."

Cameron snickers. "Wrap up. Your family doesn't need another illegitimate child."

"Fuck off," Darren barks in response. Even with

the shadows, I can tell his face is red, Cameron's words hitting too close to home.

When they start fighting, it's past time to get the hell out of there. I take the worn path toward the main door before letting myself in. Few lights are interspersed throughout the ground floor, making everything glow eerily. I make my way up the stairs slowly, so Keegan can catch up.

Before I'm even midway up the staircase, the main door opens, and a body steps through. I wait, smiling down until I realize it's not Keegan coming through, it's an elder Knight. He peers up to find me staring at him. "Miss Astor."

"Sir Jarvis. Good to see you. I didn't think any of the elders were coming in until tomorrow."

He gives me a fond smile. "We're not supposed to, but the castle is my favorite. Don't worry. I'm not peeking at anything." He climbs the stairs and walks past, taking the shallow steps two at a time. When he's only a few stairs above me, he turns, his tongue darting out to sweep over his lips. "I'm glad you made it this far, Delilah."

His words sound more ominous than praising. They makes the hair on the back of my neck stand. "Thank you," I rush out, trying to talk myself out of being paranoid. Just because a few people are unhappy about the fact that I'm here doesn't mean everyone is.

When I focus on him again, he's smiling genuinely. I brush off the weird vibes and wave goodnight to him. He retreats, slipping up the staircase silently. The castle ambiance must have me on edge.

"Delilah?" Keegan whispers.

Again, I peer toward the front door. This time, I find who I expect. "Hey," I call out, waving so he'll see me in the shadows.

He looks up, smiling, before moving forward. "I'm glad you didn't go to the rooms yet."

I wait for him where I am. He runs up to greet me, placing a kiss on my cheek before threading his arm through mine. Tugging me up the rest of the staircase, we head toward our rooms. He stops me outside mine. I'd already figured we'd sleep together, so I'm not ambushed when he takes both my hands and leads me in front of his door.

"I have a surprise for you." Reaching out, he twists the doorknob, and his door creaks open. Inside, the room is a direct replica of mine, except one key difference. Candles are lit everywhere.

"What's this?" I walk inside, turning in a circle at the plethora of candles adorning every available space. The soft glow gives his room an even more fantastical presence.

"I know I'm shitty at showing you how much I care," Keegan relays. "I get in my own way. I can be callous and cold." I peer at him, the strength in his voice only increasing as he goes. "Delilah, I don't want to be that guy for you. I want to be the guy you've seen in me since we were kids. The front I've been putting on is getting old and tiring. I've done a lot of thinking over the last two weeks, and the truth is, I've loved you so much that I wanted to save you from me. From the darkness I feel inside sometimes."

"You...love me?" I ask, hope anchoring in my chest. We've clearly come a long way recently, but I wasn't expecting this. I've been dreaming about this moment for years.

"So fucking much." He pulls me close, his huge breath expanding his chest against mine. "I was scared. I was dumb. I actively worked against you because I thought we would end up miserable like everyone else." He pulls me away at arm's length. The depth in his eyes catches my breath. "Trying to pigeonhole you, Delilah, was the worst mistake of my life. The reason we're going to work is because you don't bend to my every will. You won't fall to your knees on my every whim. You fight back," he grinds out.

His words have stolen my breath. He fractures in front of me with unshed tears. "I've loved you since we were kids, Keegan," I tell him honestly. "I've been waiting for you to say that for a very long time."

My declaration loosens something inside him. He

moves forward, capturing my lips with his. He runs his hand to the back of my head, holding me steady, his tongue delving into the deep recesses of my mouth until I'm consumed by him. He's all around me. His hands, his lips, the press of his hips against mine.

He pulls away, breathing roughly. Anticipation lays heavy between us. "I want to fuck you so bad. I want to ease all the pent-up tension between us. Taking it slow will be damn near impossible, but I'll make it good for you." He reaches up to pinch my nipple, and I moan, inching my hips toward his. "Or maybe not. You match me in so many ways. You want me pumping inside you, too, don't you?"

I place my hands on his chest, his heart beats erratically underneath my palms. This will be the easiest declaration I'll have to make. It's been coming for years, building up more and more pressure. Every single night together that we've spent for the last week has been building to this. He's not going to hold back, and I don't want him to either. "I want you everywhere, Keegan Forbes. Your cock. Your lips. Your strong hands."

He reaches behind me, scooping his hands under my ass and pulling me up his torso. I move my legs around him as he joins us at the hip and carries me to the bed. I'm well acquainted with Keegan's different levels of being turned on. He's already hard, straining through his pants. While he sets me down on the edge of the bed, I immediately work to free him. My shaking fingers fumble a few times as I slip the button through the hole and lower his zipper. He praises me, cooing my name like a prayer and a sin at the same time.

He rubs the crotch of my pants, searching for my clit through the material where he knows he'll be able to ready me in no time. Already, my panties dampen from his attention. "I'm not even nervous," I tell him as I press his jeans past his hips. "I'm just excited."

"I'm nervous," he reveals. He sinks his fingers into my hips and lifts while I lower my jeans. As soon as they're at my thighs, I sit back down and take the hem of my shirt to whisk it over my head. When it hits the floor, he slows the pace. Opening my legs at the knees, he leans back to take me in. "I want you to enjoy this, but I'm afraid I'll fuck it up, so talk to me. Be honest."

"There's no way you'll fuck this up," I tell him. I slip my hand down his front, cradling his erection. "Keegan, I want this cock inside me."

He groans. Reaching behind his back, he grabs his shirt and tears it over his head. Next, he shoves his boxers and jeans down his legs. I'm now the only one still wearing clothes. I squirm, wishing I could just take my bra and panties off, but he wraps his hands around my wrists, keeping them on the bed.

I try to pull away and frown when he won't let me

move. A bead of pre-cum forms on the tip of his dick, and I lick my lips.

"Do you want me to wear a condom? Or should we get started on this legacy we're building?"

I lift my brows, taken aback by his question. However, the full force of his eyes turns me upside down. He slips his hands to my hips, massaging me there, lulling me into a state of complete calm and serenity. "I'm all in," I tell him.

The groan that rumbles from his chest pebbles my nipples. Leaning me backward, he moves the crotch of my panties aside and slips a finger past the barrier. I drop my head back, letting him work me up until I'm moving with him. "God, you're so sexy." With his free hand, he reaches to move the cup of my bra out of the way. Sucking my nipple into his mouth, he flicks his tongue over the very tip until I'm sighing his name.

When I start moving with him, he hooks his finger inside me, and I cry out at the pinch of pleasure. In the next instant, he's pulled his finger from me, yanked my panties down, and is hovering over me on the bed. The head of his cock rests on my stomach as he leans down to kiss me. I sneak my hand between us, rubbing the head of his dick. "Fuuuck," he moans.

Propping me up, he reaches behind my back and manages to unclasp my bra. I help him remove it before he's crushing his body to mine, laying out over me as his cock aligns with my entrance.

"Is this okay?" he asks roughly.

He nudges my opening and just that slight sensation has me arching my back. I'm under no illusion that my first time will be sunshine and rainbows. However, I'm willing to practice until it is. "Yes," I promise. "Please."

Carefully, he shifts forward until the head of his dick penetrates. I bite my lip, waiting for the awful part. He asks if I'm okay before each push. I'm so turned on that even though I can feel him, it's not uncomfortable. Just before he's fully seated, however, I feel a slight pinch that makes me take a harsh breath in.

He falters, but I grind out, "Don't stop."

He makes the final push, keeping his hips still while I get used to him. "Holy shit, Dee." He breathes out, his hot breath caressing my cheek.

So much for fucking me like he said. The fact that he can be this careful proves to me how far Keegan Forbes has come.

I wrap my arms around him, reaching up his back while still trying to get used to the feeling of fullness. My hands work up his spine, trailing my fingertips along his muscles. I lift my hips gingerly, and he groans. He follows my lead, not urging me to move faster but going at my pace. The pinching feeling stays for a little while but eventually evaporates the more we explore. Reaching between us, he rubs my clit while making slow, shallow strokes. Then, it's not like a science experiment anymore. I'm not trying to find the spot where it can feel good because it *all* feels good. "Keegan," I sigh.

"Let me know if I go too far."

The more he winds my body up, the more I reach my hips up to meet his. My body trembles, and my toes curl. He presses his lips together as he works me over. "God, Keegan," I groan at the mix of pleasure flowing through me. By now, I'm well acquainted with clitoral stimulation but adding the pressure of his dick amplifies everything. He knows exactly the pace to push forward. "Oh, God, Keegan," I pant. My hips jerk, but he stays the pace, the rhythm of his nimble fingers taking me to new heights. "Ohhh," I breathe out. The tension inside me pulls taut until I'm walking a thin line of utter perfection. "Yes, yes," I repeat. A second later, my walls constrict around his cock, and I cry out, moving against him as I climax.

Euphoria sets in for several blissful moments. Afterward, I sink down onto the bed. All pinches and pain are gone as I revel in my tingling limbs and spent body.

Keegan leans over, whispering, "That was beautiful."

He lets me lay there in my state of pleasure until I come back around, eager to give him the same thing I just experienced. "I want to watch you," I tell him.

He licks his lips, his hooded eyes welcoming the invitation. He starts slow, but I urge him forward, pressing up into him. The more I get into it, the faster he moves. He slides inside me, his strokes sure and confident. "Oh, baby, yes," he praises. "So tight. Fuck, I can't get enough." He starts to shake. I sink my fingers into his skin as he increases the pressure, searching out his own pleasure. "Fuck me, Dee. God," he groans. The bed creaks underneath us as he explodes. He grinds out his release against me, his cock spasming.

I link my ankles around his ass, pulling toward me to rock with him until he drops his forehead to mine.

"I'm never leaving," he says. "I think I'll stay here forever."

My head drops back on the bed, and I laugh. "We're never getting work done again, are we?"

His chest rattles with humor. "Not if I have anything to say about it." He meets my gaze. Raw and honest blue eyes latch to mine. "You're perfect."

I tried for a long time to make people think I was. Maybe I was wrong to attempt something so utterly undefined. However, in this moment, being perfect for Keegan is all I want.

eegan's fingers trace down my arm. I'm going to need all the makeup in the world to make it look like I got a good night's sleep instead of what I was actually doing. Grinning, I turn my head to stare at Keegan as memories of last night, this morning, *and* this afternoon filter through my foggy brain. I'm now intimately acquainted with all of Keegan Forbes. I doubt there's anything he could say that would shock me anymore.

I'd say I was missing out by not giving in to Keegan before, but on the other hand, he understands me so much better now. We're finally at a place where we're not working against each other.

"What's that look for?" he asks.

I shrug. "Just thinking..."

"Just thinking how much you love my dick?"

I shake my head, but my cheeks heat anyway because he's not wrong.

He slides his fingertips along my cheekbone. "Because I was just thinking how much I enjoyed last night." He gives me a small smile, and there's just something in his blue eyes that's akin to an apology. "You were well worth the wait."

"I know," I tell him, smirking. I press a smacking kiss to his cheek and start to get up. He grabs my arm, yanking me back down to the bed where he hovers over me.

"Is that so?"

I giggle like my middle school crush is picking on me. In a way, he is. Keegan has always been my crush, even through the difficult times. As we got older, the feelings only intensified. "I don't blame you for running away from me," I tell him. He cocks his head to the side, the smile slipping from his face. "You and I are a lot to take in."

"I never stopped caring about you though."

"I know that."

He leans down, pressing his lips to my neck in a slow caress. I arch, giving him plenty of room to explore.

A knock sounds on the door, and I freeze momentarily before trying to flee the bed. He holds me in place before calling out, "Yes?"

"Refreshments, Sir."

"Come in," he beckons.

"Keegan," I growl, looking at the sheets wrapped around me in panic. We're definitely in a compromising position.

"It's the waitstaff," he assures me. "They won't even blink an eye."

"I know that," I mumble as the door opens. There's such a thing called modesty though. I don't want to be on display, but it's too late. The older gentleman enters the room without a glance toward the bed. He keeps his gaze either on the tray or straight ahead.

Placing the tray on the bedside table, he announces, "Tea and a few bakery items for you, Sir."

"Thank you," Keegan tells him, sitting up. The white sheets fall to his lap, and my stomach flips. Keegan, however, doesn't even look down to make sure he's covered.

The staff member leaves the room without another word, and the tension in the air leaves with him. I check the clock in the room and sigh. I have to meet the models at the dock in just over an hour.

"Eat something before you run off to put the rest of us Fledglings to shame," he taunts, handing me a muffin.

I sniff the browned top, the banana aroma tickling my senses. "Mmm," I murmur. It smells like heaven.

"I'm about to take it to go, so I can show all of you up." I place it on the table closest to me and throw on my clothes from last night. Before I pick up my banana muffin, I kneel on the bed and lean over to kiss Keegan who's propped up on the bed like he's a king. He wraps his free hand around my neck, pulling me closer. "Love you, Dee. See you later?"

"Later," I promise.

No one is in the hallway to perform the walk of shame for, so I easily slip into my room unnoticed to find the same tray of goodies on my bedside table. I wonder what the waitstaff member thought when I wasn't in my own room, but in Keegan's. Oh well. My father always told me that what other people think of me is none of my business.

I take a shower and prep for the day, being painstakingly careful in applying my makeup to hide the shadows under my eyes. I dress in a plain, navy-blue dress that swings around my knees. It's not the beautiful dress I'll wear tonight, but it has just the right amount of fun and business flavor to get through this morning with.

Taking a few bites out of the muffin, I set it back down only to find a note on my breakfast tray. I pull it out, opening it to find a personal request for a meeting. The note says Knight A...maybe? It could be a J, a B. Really, the signature is hard to decipher. I check my watch, deciding I have just enough time to get the models settled in before attending the meeting. The elder Knights will already be on the island by the time the meeting takes place. Why this Knight would want to meet with me before the party, I have no idea.

My veins turn cold. Unless someone complained about me again? Cameron, because I won't have sex with him?

For a brief moment, my mind tells me Keegan, but I flick that nasty thought away. We're much better now. There's no way he's trying to get me in trouble with the Knights again. He understands why it's so important to me now.

I'll just have to wait to find out what the meeting is about. Like I need another thing to worry over today.

I hurry down to the dock just as the boat carrying the models pulls in. The same captain we had yesterday is at the helm, however, he looks like he's in a much better mood. He's all smiles, lending the girls a hand as they step off the boat and onto the wood dock. I wave at them from the winding walk that leads to the castle, and a few of them wave back. Honestly, we did a great job choosing the models. They're all going to kill it in their angel costumes in a few hours.

They form a semi-circle around me, their chins tipped toward the sky, no doubt looking at the massive building at my back. It's a sight to see, for sure. Some of their mouths hang open while others squeal in awe at the place. I only hope they feel that way when they have to kowtow to the guests later. Their gift bags are already assembled in the basement room I acquired as their dressing room.

I'm about to start addressing them when another figure gets off the boat. I do a double take at the familiar form. I'm aware of every name on the guest list, and Tim's certainly not on it.

I push past some of the girls to ward him off, calling for the captain to wait as he starts to untie his tethering ropes from the dock. "What are you doing here?" I whisper yell as I approach Tim.

He glares at me. "You never met me the other day."

I stare blankly at him. I have no idea what he's talking about. "You know, I kind of thought you were normal, but this is a little much. Are you here for me?"

He reaches for my hand, but I step away. Sighing, he stares. "I gave you that note."

Oh, shit. I completely forgot about it. I didn't even bother to read the note because I've been so preoccupied with party planning and Keegan.

"Dee, you don't know the whole story about what's been going on. I needed to tell you."

My insides squeeze. "You can tell me when I get back to campus. You're not even supposed to be here,

Tim." I glare at the captain accusingly. He was most definitely not on his approved guest list either.

"It's something you need to know now. There was a bet, Delilah. As soon as it got around campus that you were a virgin, everyone started making bets about who was going to take your virginity. Whoever does is set to make a substantial amount of money."

I recoil, flabbergasted Tim would even be aware of the whole betting scheme some of the guys on campus had. Honestly, it's just like them, but no one took it seriously except for their feeble attempts to ask me out. Cameron is the only one who talked to me in person. "How'd you hear about it?" He peers away, and a sliver of ice hardens over my spine. "You were in on it? That's why you asked me to go out sometime that one day?"

"I wasn't going to take the money," Tim argues. "I just saw that you were suddenly with that dickhead, and I got worried he was using you."

"That dickhead is my boyfriend. He's been my on again off again boyfriend since we were kids. He didn't —he's not participating in some bet," I scoff.

Tim shakes his head. "If you trust any of the rich assholes that go to your school, you're delusional."

"Keegan has enough money," I protest. "He doesn't need to win some stupid bet about my virginity, and I guess it's not just the rich boys at my school

I have to watch out for, is it?" I shake my head. I'm good at reading people, and it's so damn evident that Tim was in on it. "Newsflash," I tell him, stepping closer to get in his face. "The deed's already done, so if you think that by showing up here and warning me about this bet that I'll be so thankful I'll just bend over for you right here, you're wrong. Get a life, Tim."

He flinches, his eyes shadowing over. His throat works as he eyes me. "Fine," he finally concedes. He takes another look before turning and walking away, head lowered. My stomach tightens, and a moment of guilt pings inside me. What if he was only trying to warn me?

"Get on the boat, boy," the captain demands. "I ain't got all day."

Before I know it, the boat is moving away from the dock. The engine growls to change course, and I stare after it, Tim peering right back at me.

I close my eyes and breathe out. I'll deal with him later. Apologize, *maybe*. It's best he left the island because if anyone saw him here, I'd get in trouble. How he even knew where to find me is another thing. Stalker much?

My stomach bottoms out, but I dismiss that thought right away. Tim doesn't seem like the kind of guy who would cum in a condom and put it in a bouquet of flowers. He seemed so hurt after I yelled at him, like a kicked puppy.

I breathe out, trying to get myself under control. Behind me, the voices of the ladies grow louder, so I turn, plastering on my "I'm good" face and leading them around to the various areas of the castle they'll be expected to be schmoozing in tonight. While they're checking out the dinner patio area, I pull my phone out and text Keegan. **I need to talk to you.**

He hasn't played me. I'm sure of it. But he's known about the bet. Maybe that's why he fought Cameron and Tim. If he can get his hand on the list of bettors, we can send it to my dad to cross-check with anything we found in the bouquet and card.

The sky starts to glow with that orange-pink hue, signaling the start of evening. I check my watch and hurriedly gather the girls together to take them downstairs to the dressing room. The elders will be coming shortly, and after that, the boats will start arriving with the guests who were able to make it through the treasure hunt style opening.

It was a genius idea. If the invited guests weren't smart enough to figure out the clues, they'll never find themselves at the special dock to take the ferries over. That way, we can promote having only the best and brightest partying with the Knights on this special day. The Knights love exclusivity. They'll be tickled to death with the outcome, and plus, instant small talk accomplished. Everyone will be discussing how they made it to the docks.

As we walk into the dressing room, the amount of high-pitched screaming I hear from the models spying their goodie bags is enough to make my ears ring. They start pulling items out, jaws dropping. "Be ready in one hour," I call out, trying to talk over the melee.

"We'll be ready!" a pretty redhead answers.

I make a mental note to get down here fifteen minutes before I'd scheduled myself to, just so I can make sure they're all on time. Mrs. Dupont will also be watching out for them, but I want to pull my own weight when it comes to the girls.

As I slip from the room, I close the door behind me and pull out my phone. I have a missed call from Keegan, so I call him back as I stride down the hallway. I have to meet the Knight who left me the note in the billiard room before I can go upstairs and get ready. Keegan's phone goes to voicemail. My heart beats faster as I search for the room I vaguely remember seeing on my tour. I leave him a message telling him that Tim showed up at the island, but not to worry because I sent him away. Then, I tell him my idea of using the bettor list to narrow down our suspects. "Love you," I tell him, ending the voicemail.

Finally, I find the billiard room and take a deep

breath. I fan my face to make it look as if I haven't been running around for the past hour and make sure my dress is in place before knocking on the door.

A voice calls out, "Come in."

I force a smile to my face and push the heavy wooden door open. The Knight stands straight after taking a pool shot. He sets the cue down. "Ahh, Miss Astor."

My voice almost falters. I didn't expect it to be *him* of all people. "Hello."

"It's good to see you. All of the party details seem like they are coming together."

"They are, Sir," I tell him, making sure my voice stays steady and even.

Just to my right, the bookcase swings open on a hinge. Another Knight steps out, and my heart starts to race when I recognize him too. I guess this party brings out the most elite members.

"We're ready for her," his even, solemn voice states. *We? Who's we?*

The other man strides over, placing his arm carefully around my shoulder. "Just this way, Miss Astor."

"What's this about?" I ask. It's not as if I can refuse to accompany someone as high up as these Knights, but I am sort of busy. "I have a lot of party duties to attend to."

"Don't worry about that," he says, his fingers slipping down my bare shoulder. My head starts to pound, but he maneuvers behind me, his front against my back and leaves me no other choice but to head toward the secret door. I step in front of it and find a short set of winding footsteps.

Flickering lights cast part of the stone stairwell in shadow.

"Don't delay, Miss Astor. We're all busy here, and we're looking forward to celebrating Devil's Night with you."

I step onto the first stone stair. A burst of cold air cascades over my skin. I can feel the body behind me so I continue my descent, my footsteps echoing around the narrow walkway.

"Where are we going?"

He makes a sound of amusement in the back of his throat. "Into the dungeon."

CHAPTER 20

I descend the curving staircase, sandwiched between the two elders. My pulse pounds in my ears. Before me, an archway opens up at the bottom. Little by little, the scene in the dungeon comes into view, making me stop on the very last stair.

Figures in hooded robes stand in a circle. Shadows flicker across the low ceiling from the burning torches slid into metal brackets around the room.

"Just a little further," the prominent elder at my back prompts.

I turn to face him. His eyes aren't nearly as friendly anymore. "I have things to do," I say confidently. Everything in me is telling me I should escape. I wished I'd gotten ahold of Keegan to ask him if he also had to attend a meeting. It would certainly calm my nerves to know all of the other Knights are going through the same thing. Maybe that's why I couldn't get ahold of Keegan? "Surely whatever this is can wait."

He lifts his chin. "Are you disobeying a direct order from an elder?"

I swallow, panic still rising even with my attempt to quell it. Maybe this is all part of the Devil's Night shenanigans? Maybe they're trying to play a joke on me? Night of mischief, right? "No, Sir."

Turning back, I step onto the rock floor. The room looks every bit the quintessential dungeon, something my mind would conjure up if I were reading about castles and places where powerful people keep prisoners.

I lift my chin high, trying not to betray the fear coursing through me. If this is a rite of passage to become a full-fledged Knight, I have to pass.

Taking a deep breath, the circle closes in around me. They're all wearing matching black masks, the prop we picked out for our Devil's Night theme. It's like being surrounded by a number of princes from hell. The hoods, the robes, they're all indistinguishable from another. I turn in a circle and find that even the two who escorted me down here are now dressed the same. I can't tell who anyone is now.

I wait until I'm spoken to. They're in the driver's seat, and it won't do any good for me to try to guess whatever situation they're putting me in. Is this another trial, perhaps? Something to prove my worth. Or worse? Maybe this is how I get kicked out, the culmination of Keegan's complaint coming to a head. They don't suffer outsiders or people who won't work with them. I could be on a boat within ten minutes, being shipped away from the Knights forever.

Or maybe, they've finally decided to pull the plug on the idea of the first woman Knight. No reason needed.

I peer around, searching for my father. If that's what's happening here, I would hope he'd have given me a heads up. I find nothing distinguishable about them though. Their eyes scour me from head-to-toe, all varying in shades of darkness due to the low light.

I'm about to break first when a voice pours out into the small room, an air of authority dripping from every syllable. "Clearly," it rings. "The honor should be mine."

A bunch of disgusted dissents rise up, making the hair on the back of my neck stand. "You would think that."

I turn, trying to search out the owner of the second voice, only to find that the circle has tightened in around me. If this is a prank, they're doing a hell of a job. I feel like a kitten in the midst of a pack of tigers. Every instinct in my body tells me to claw my way out.

"The prize will be dealt out as the others. Vivere triumpho."

"Vivere triumpho," they all repeat. The Knights motto rings through my ears as I try to guess its meaning as it pertains to me. *To live in triumph.*

"Begin," the same voice dictates.

The crowd of cloaked men hover like dark skies. My skin crawls in response like ants scurrying over my skin.

"My yacht."

"200 acres of oil rich land."

"My spot on the board."

One by one, they go around in a circle. Their statements mean little to me except for their high value. Everyone offers something up that would be very desirable to others.

"We can do better than that," a fierce voice barks.

"Maybe if we had incentive," a masculine voice purrs.

"Yes, dear. Do take off your dress."

A thunderbolt of fear strikes me in the chest. "What?" I rasp out.

Without warning, a body slides up behind me. In one motion, he unzips my dress from behind. I cross my chest to keep the top up, but he grabs the shoulders and tries to force it down. I struggle, but another figure moves forward, grabs my hands out of the way, and before I know it, my dress is pooled at my feet.

I stand in the middle of the Knight elders in nothing but my bra and panties, stripped of dignity.

They move in close. "What a prize indeed."

My vision blurs. My heart beats as if it wants to escape my chest. I turn, trying to find a way out. They're so close now, shoulder-to-shoulder, so there's no path of escape.

"My house in the Hamptons."

"Your wife will kill you," a Knight laughs.

"I'll offer her up too."

Groans rise up like sex-drenched webs of need.

A man clears his throat. "To take the most beautiful flower warrants an enormous sacrifice." I know the voice. It's the same one who met me in the billiard room. Nausea clenches my stomach.

"Ten million."

Guffaws litter the air. "We don't play in money," an angry voice chastises.

A growl rips through the room, threading through my veins like needles. "My third best company then. I need that taste." A gloved hand extends toward my mid-section, fingers flexing. "That sweet virginal pussy."

I inhale a sharp breath. Puzzle pieces click together in

abstract horror. They're having an auction for me. Well, not me. Not specifically. They want my virgin cunt, that's not even virginal anymore. Keegan took care of that almost every hour on the hour only a few hours ago.

"You will not touch me," I seethe.

Snickers echo around the chamber, coming back to me with double the intensity, weighing my body down. "But we will."

"*One* of us will," a growly voice adds.

Before he's even done saying that, someone offers, "The patent for my latest invention."

"Mmm," an appreciative voice sounds.

"I don't need the cunt," another says. "I'll give up my father's ruby ring for her red lips wrapped around my cock."

"Have you given head before, Delilah?" a sultry voice asks.

"My Rolls Royce to watch," another adds.

"Second that with my mint condition Jaguar, E-Type."

My harsh breaths fill the room in the midst of their offers. Inside, I'm trembling like a leaf. Hot breath hits my back, and I sly away only to come face-to-face with a Knight who grabs my hips, tugging me toward him. "My construction company for her to ride my face."

I squirm out of his grip. "Let go of me."

"You've been chosen, Delilah. You have something we all want. The choice isn't yours anymore."

"Fuck you."

Groans sound again. "I'll settle for jerking off with my fingers inside her."

I whirl toward the voice, pushing the chest of the man who said it. "You disgust me. You all do."

"I thought you wanted to be a Knight?"

Fury laps at me. "Did you give up your body to become one?" I counter. I should've known something like this would happen. They're all animals.

"We all gave up something, and we've determined this is your one, true offering to the Knights of Arcadia."

"I am not sleeping with any of you."

"You don't have to like it," another voice adds.

Another voice chuckles. "In fact, I'd prefer it if she didn't."

More harsh laughter. The despicable words leaving these Knights' mouths make me shiver. "Dad?" I call out.

The answering cackles send a ball of ice to my stomach. "He's not here, Delilah. Of course."

My mind races ahead, trying to figure out what to say to get out of this. Should I tell them I'm no longer a virgin? Will that make it worse?

"Mr. Forbes?" I ask desperately. "I'm Keegan's. You promised."

A figure moves forward, and I spin toward it. A cherry red tongue presses against curved lips. "That's why I said you should be mine by right. I had no idea you were still untouched Delilah. If Keegan hadn't said anything to me..."

"My father will never forgive you."

"Your father knows what it's like to be a Knight. You think he hasn't participated in games like this?"

Opposing images collide in my head. Chaos settles in until I can't think clearly. Half my mind rejects what I know to be happening, overpowering any rational thought. It's like everything is in a haze.

"Shall we choose now? Or do we need more incentive?"

"You're doing all this for virgin pussy?" I ask incredulously. "Couldn't you just find someone willing?"

"Vivere triumpho, Delilah," the main voice rings out. "Sometimes it's not enough to be given, sometimes it's best to take."

I roar, throwing myself at the figure closest to me, trying to push past him. Hands scramble to grab me. Others shout not to hurt me, but I'm sure it's not because they're worried about causing me pain. They probably want a clean canvas to defile me.

"Just lie back and take it, Delilah. You'll be a Knight afterward, and no one will have to know beyond the men in this room."

Fingers sink into my skin, and I grimace. "Give up a piece of me. No fucking way. Not for you. Not for anyone."

I was a fool to think I could change them. I never thought of anything as heinous as this existed though. An auction for my virginity, willingly or not. It's despicable.

"But that's what we do, Miss Astor. We give up ourselves for the greater good. You'll be rewarded handsomely with Knighthood."

But I'll be giving up so much more. I still struggle against restraining hands. "I don't want any part of this."

"Do you remember what was said the night of the first trial? Once you start, you see it through. You can't stop now."

"The hell I can't. If you so much as touch me, I'll bring down hell on the Knights. I'll expose all of your secrets. I saw some of you," I continue, my mind reeling with the thoughts of the high-powered men in this room. Positions of authority. Rich men who have access to millions and millions. And one of them offered up his own wife?

Disgusting.

My world crumbles around me. Dad told me to be strong, but my weaknesses are on full display. I feel like the jester at court, everyone laughing for how naive I've been.

"Hold her. She'll see reason eventually."

"We can play pass the virgin. Spread her wide, mouths only. She'll come around. All the dirty little whores do."

A hand supports my back as two of the cloaked figures kneel to grab my legs. Panic is at pre-volcano eruption levels, gurgling inside me. I kick out, managing to connect the heel of my shoe to the mask of one of the Knights.

His mask sits askew, and I growl as I recognize his face. More illustrious bastards. If the world only knew.

Survival kicks in. The Knights are too far gone. They're not just some old boys club where they promise each other favors in business, helping them all to stay on top of a volatile market. They're so much more sinister than that.

Power corrupts. It bleeds vile, vile things. It's settled into the heart of these men, and I'm currently in the middle. One lone girl. One lone fight.

I'm not going down like this.

I kick out again. A second after I connect, a roar of pain echoes through the room. I wiggle, twisting and turning, trying to free myself from their grasps. The figure on my left drops my hand, and my momentum sends me down, causing the others to lose their grip.

I spy an opening in the circle, fighting my way out. Elbows, kicks, headbutts. I'm like a rabid animal who desperately seeks light. My hands break free, then my torso. I send a few donkey kicks backward, using my long, lean ballet legs to connect with more men before I scramble on all fours and then sprint.

If I get to the stairs, I'm free.

The tunnel is tight, they won't all be able to fight me at once. With their cumbersome robes, I should be able to run up the steps faster than the rest.

Where to go after that though? I don't know. I have only one focus right now.

I run, my hands pumping at my sides, my feet propelling me forward. I hit the first step and a hand scratches down my shoulder and wraps around my bra strap. I keep going, keep fighting. The strap snaps, and I bolt up the stairs, taking them two at a time, praying that years of balance and grace will carry me even further this time.

I spring into the billiard room, bypassing the table with balls still erratically placed when I interrupted *his* game.

Once out into the hallway, I run and run. My footsteps and harsh breaths make me an easy identifiable target, but I keep going. Taking one hallway, then the next. Thunderous footsteps sound behind me, but I keep going.

Ducking under a low archway, I find a different area of the castle. A much older one. I dodge stone pillars, my low heels digging into dirt now. To my right, I spy the night sky through a scattering of stone supports.

A tunnel narrows ahead of me, and I push through, running blindly with just the hint of light from the overhead stars. The silhouette of a bush denotes the end of the tunnel, and I find myself bursting free of the exit, branches scraping against my face.

Now that we're on dirt, I don't hear their footsteps following, but I have no doubt they're there. They're not going to let me get away with this.

The cold air pricks my skin. My ragged breaths only worsen as I escape. I could run out into the forest or— As I round the bend, I spot a boat getting ready to leave the dock. I have a focus now. A plan. If I can just get on the boat, the captain will take me to safety. I can hide. I'll call my parents. I'll tell them what happened. No way will Dad stand for this. Or if he does, I'll take the Knights down without his help.

Eden will be on my side. She'll fight for me. This is just the type of cause she'd use to take down the bitter upstart old douches, she would say.

I'm getting closer and closer. The boat is a few feet from the dock now. I can jump, and I might just—

A hand grips my shoulder from behind. My heels twist underneath me, and I go down hard. My hands and knees scrape against the wooden dock, and I cry out in pain. The boat's motor drowns me out. Burnt oil assaults my nostrils as it gets further away.

"You really shouldn't have done that, Delilah."

The guy who caught up to me heaves me forward. I'm still in pain that I don't realize what he's doing until I'm falling.

For a split second, I'm in a freefall. Fear stealing my thoughts. I don't know where I am until I plunge into water. The freezing river steals my breath. Panic claws at me, and I frantically reach through the dark water, searching for the surface.

I'm thrown back in time. Horror closes in and terror binds my throat, making it start to close.

I need air. I need air.

Keegan, I think. He saved me last time.

My hand breaks the surface, and I propel myself upward in relief. I'm able to gasp a single, painful breath until I'm pushed under once more.

Fingertips dig into my scalp, and I scream, releasing all the air I just took in. Another force pushes me down further and further. My mouth opens to yell again. Bubbles release instead, and when there's no more air, I end up choking on water.

Pure hysterics take over. No matter how hard I try, I can't reach the surface. My hair tangles around me like shadowy spiderwebs.

Voices rise up. Shouts. Alarm.

I have a fleeting thought of hope, but no one comes. Not even Keegan, my savior. My love.

The edges of my vision turn dark, creeping inward little by little as my lungs ache for air. Stars dot my vision, and in the midst of them, I spy Keegan, covered in a mist-like dream. He stands at the end of the dock, frowning down at me.

In the next second, he's gone. My vision narrows further, tiny needles of river water freeze my skin, making my lungs seize up.

It's as if I can feel life slowly draining from me.

My movements become slow, labored. In the last few seconds of consciousness, I spy my limbs floating at my sides, and I'm unable to make them move anymore.

Blinding pain, and a moment of innate calmness, passes before there's nothing more.

Nothing.

I'm dust in the wind. A lifeless vessel drifting with the river current.

I. Am. Gone.

E. M. Moore is a USA Today Bestselling author of Contemporary and Paranormal Romance. She's drawn to write within the teen and college-aged years where her characters get knocked on their asses, torn inside out, and put back together again by their first loves. Whether it's in a fantastical setting where human guards protect the creatures of the night or a realistic high school backdrop where social cliques rule the halls, the emotions are the same. Dark. Twisty. Angsty. Raw.

When Erin's not writing, you can find her dreaming up vacations for her family, watching murder mystery shows, or dancing in her kitchen while she pretends to cook.